A Dream for Two

Kate Goldman

A Dream for Two

Published by Kate Goldman

Copyright © 2014 by Kate Goldman

ISBN 978-1-50312-086-0

First printing, 2014

www.KateGoldmanBooks.com

PRINTED IN THE UNITED STATES OF AMERICA

Dedication

I want to dedicate this book to my beloved husband, who makes every day in my life worthwhile. Thank you for believing in me when nobody else does, giving me encouragement when I need it the most, and loving me simply for being myself.

Table of Contents

Chapter 1

Elise Roberts tucked her dark bangs behind her ears and blinked her hazel eyes rapidly. Surely she had misheard? She was sitting in her boss' office. Outside the sun was shining, the sky was a brilliant shade of blue. It was supposed to be a beautiful day yet here he was saying words like "downscaling."

"It's nothing personal, Elise," Colin Sanders continued. He was a heavyset man with a quickly receding hairline which made him appear much older than his thirty-five years.

"I've worked here for five years," Elise blurted. She tightened her hands which were neatly clasped together on her lap. She had thought she was the model employee. Ever since she'd graduated from high school she had worked for Curtis Cleaning Products. She was based in their offices, carrying out basic administrative duties. A couple of people she went to school with worked on the factory floor.

Elise was never late for work. She was courteous and kind and wasn't adverse to working overtime when it was required. She was always well dressed with a friendly smile upon her pretty face. Like most girls raised in the South, Elise had been brought up to be graceful and well mannered, qualities which her grandmother had fiercely instilled in her.

"I know," Colin nodded. "And here at Curtis Cleaning Products we are indebted to your loyal service over those years."

"Then...why are you letting me go?"

"Like I said, downscaling," Colin reiterated. "The company has had some tough months recently and we need to cut costs where we can."

Elise held back tears. She was just a cost that could be cut? Did she not matter as a person? As a colleague?

"I'm really sorry," Colin stood up and extended his hand across the desk towards Elise. Their meeting was drawing to a close. Still blindsided by everything, Elise numbly shook his hand. As she walked back to her small desk nothing felt real. She felt as though she were in a dream, or living someone else's life. This wasn't her life. She hadn't just been fired. She had a good, stable job in a local company. She had her whole future mapped out.

But it started to feel real as Elise stepped out into the morning sunshine. The golden rays caressed her skin but the sun's presence did little to alleviate her mood. Carrying her modest box full of personal belongings, Elise hurried over to her car. She just wanted to leave, to get away from there.

A Dream for Two

Once in her car Elise flicked on the stereo and the new Claire Parry song came on. Leaning back, she listened to the fast tempo of the melody, the natural brightness in the singer's voice. Elise had always found solace in music. It was music which had helped her through some of the toughest times in her life. Turning up the volume she maneuvered out of the parking lot, away from Curtis Cleaning Products. Her life had been flipped in the space of just one morning but for the brief drive home she wouldn't care. She'd just wind down the windows, let the wind whip her hair and sing along to her favorite artist as loudly as she could.

***

"What do you mean they let you go?" Elise's grandmother paused with the jug of iced tea in her hand, poised to pour into her granddaughter's glass.

"They just let me go," Elise told her again. Since getting home she'd cast off the smart office wear she'd so carefully dressed in that morning and was now in sweatpants and a white t-shirt.

"But why?" her grandmother persisted. "You're such a good little worker!"

"He said something about downscaling," Elise shrugged.

"I'd like to downscale him!" her grandmother seethed, placing a free hand on her hip.

"I just don't know what I'm going to do," Elise sighed despairingly. "All I've known is working there."

"You'll figure it out," her grandmother promised warmly as she finally poured the iced tea. The ice in the glass tinkled magically and swirled within the liquid.

***

Elise wasn't so sure she would figure it out. She'd never been great at sorting her life out. Ever since her parents died in a car accident when she was eleven she had lived with her grandmother. As a little girl she'd had dreams of being a singer. She'd listen to her mother's old albums and sing along at the top of her voice. Her parents would watch admiringly and tell her that she had the makings of a star. And Elise believed them. Each time they told her that she was special, that she had something, she believed them. And then they died and everything changed.

Idly Elise strummed the guitar she was holding. She was resting beneath a willow tree in her grandmother's backyard. Normally she'd be taking inventory back at the factory but not today. Today she had nowhere to go and nowhere to be.

"You can still play a nice tune on that," her grandmother said, squinting into the sunlight as she wandered slowly into the garden.

"At least I can do something," Elise muttered, feeling melancholy.

"Don't be so defeatist," her grandmother chastised her. Annabelle Roberts was a strong woman, she'd had to be. She raised her daughter as a single mother, then lost her and had to repeat everything all over again with her only granddaughter. She was warm and kind but could be formidable when she had to be.

"I just don't know what I'm supposed to do with my life," Elise sighed. Then she repeated the sentence, but this time she sang it along with a tune she'd just made up. She strummed along on her guitar and it actually made her feel better.

"You always had a talent for music," Annabelle smiled fondly. "Your parents saw that in you. That's why they bought you that guitar."

Elise looked down at the instrument she was holding. She remembered the Christmas her parents had presented her with it, the Christmas right before they died. For almost a year after that she refused to play it, refused to connect with the memory. But then something happened. Elise realized that music could heal her. Through the guitar she could unleash all her sadness, all her anger, in the medium of song.

"Maybe that's what you should be doing with your life," Annabelle nodded at the guitar.

"What, Grandma? Busk for small change down by the mall?" Elise asked sarcastically. Her mood was still extremely sour thanks to the morning's events.

"No," Annabelle shook her head and her old eyes glistened with the arrival of a great idea.

"You should be like those singers on the radio."

Elise shook her head dismissively.

"I'm not good enough, and even if I were, I'm too old now."

"Too old!" Annabelle almost choked on her words. "Sweet girl, you're only twenty-three. You've got the rest of your life ahead of you. Don't get jaded now. See losing your job as the push you needed to get you in the right direction. You should be a star, Elise Roberts, everyone knows it but you."

Elise continued to strum her guitar as her grandmother's words slowly sank in. She had always dreamed of playing her own music to an audience, of having her own album, even a tour. But she thought that those dreams belonged to other people, to people who had their parents around to support and encourage them.

"Think about it," Annabelle advised before heading back into the house. The afternoon heat was always too much for her.

***

Elise had been thinking about what her grandmother had said but it all seemed so abstract. How did anybody go about becoming a pop star? You could hardly walk into somewhere with a résumé and ask to be made famous. Or was that exactly how it happened? Elise had no idea. Where she came from, it wasn't exactly the norm to go chasing big dreams. Most people were content with regular jobs and regular dreams.

"What's that?" Elise spotted the bus ticket on the table as she sat down for breakfast. It was strategically placed in the center of the plaid tablecloth so that she wouldn't miss it.

"That's for you," her grandmother called from by the stove where she was making fresh blueberry pancakes. Elise reached forward and picked up the ticket. As she scrutinized its details she saw that it was a ticket to New York, leaving the following day.

Still holding the ticket, she asked her grandmother, "Are you going on a trip?"

"Nope," Annabelle shook her head of curled grey hair. "You are."

"What?" Elise's voice rose in surprise.

Her grandmother approached the table with the fresh pancakes.

"You are going to New York," she told her granddaughter. "You're going to take that old six-string and you're going to follow your dreams."

"But Grandma—"

"I won't hear any objections," Annabelle warned, pointing her spatula at Elise. "It's what your folks would have wanted."

"I can't just pack up and leave you!" Elise insisted. "Besides, this is just a one-way ticket."

"You can and you will," Annabelle said sternly, dishing out the pancakes onto Elise's plate.

"I will be just fine, I can take care of myself, I've been doing it all my life and I've gotten pretty good at it! And there is no ticket home, honey, because when you come back it won't be on some bus, it will be flying first class like the star you are."

"I don't know," Elise eyed the ticket dubiously. Butterflies had already begun to flutter in her stomach at the thought of going to New York.

"Me and your parents, we always saw you as the brightest star," Annabelle said as she sat down across from her, a warm smile pulled across her plump cheeks.

"And then you lost them and you forgot how special you were. Which is understandable. But if I don't help you find your way again, I'll know I failed you. You have a gift, Elise. A gift you should share with the world. The songs you write are beautiful and moving. It would be a shame if I was the only one to ever hear them."

Elise was still staring at the ticket.

"Okay," she nodded slowly. "I'll go. After all, I've got nothing to lose."

***

Elise barely slept that night. She tossed and turned and wondered what New York would be like. Would the people there be kind and friendly or would they exist in their own world? Could she exist there? She was a Southern girl from a small town, what if she wasn't up to living in the big city?

When sleep failed to come Elise crept out of bed and picked up her beloved guitar which rested by her headboard. Quietly she strummed a few notes and sang a bittersweet melody she made up there and then about the bravery needed to follow your dreams. When Elise finished singing she quickly scribbled down the notes and lyrics for the song in her old notebook. Flicking back through the pages she found many songs she had written over the years, but none had been written recently. None until that night. It seemed that even the promise of adventure had been enough to reignite her creative instincts.

As the first rays of sunlight crept in beneath her curtains Elise's bags were already packed. Her guitar was locked in its case and her notebook was tucked safely between her two favorite pairs of jeans. She was ready to get on that bus, to follow her dream.

"So are you doing this?" Annabelle asked as she helped Elise load her stuff into her car so that they could drive to the bus station.

"Yeah," Elise grinned enthusiastically, hope rising high in her chest. "I'm doing this."

Chapter 2

It was the noise which first shocked Elise. New York was an impossibly loud city. She pulled her bag along towards an apartment listing she'd found in the newspaper. As she walked, her ears were assaulted by a cacophony of car horns, jackhammers and raised voices.

And it was busy. On the road cars idled bumper to bumper as drivers impatiently waited for the lights to change. Even on the sidewalk people hurried along by the dozens, hundreds even. Elise lost count of the times she'd been shoved aside by someone desperate to pass her by. No one smiled, no one offered to help her with her bag. She was clearly a long way from home.

Finally she arrived at the address stated in the newspaper. As she stood outside the building she reread the listing to ensure she was at the right place. Her heart sank when she realized she was.

Elise was standing outside a four-story building. Half of the windows were boarded up, the other half were so dirty that you couldn't even see through them. The listing said "a city location in an apartment share perfect for first timers to New York." Elise took a deep breath and hauled her bag up the few steps which led to the front door.

***

"Rent is five hundred dollars a month, with two months paid up front," a harassed-looking man told her as he unlocked the apartment door.

"The others are out at work at the moment," he explained. Elise peered past him into the small space. She could see a sofa which had been utilized into a bed, a kitchen and the door to what she guessed was the bathroom. She wasn't sure how one person could live there, let alone three.

"I'm here because of my music," Elise blurted nervously, tapping the guitar case currently strapped to her back.

"Sure you are," the man gave her a deliberately false grin.

"Five hundred dollars," he pointed a grime-covered finger at Elise. "If you're late on rent I kick you out, don't think you can win me over with some sob story. I've heard 'em all."

He handed Elise a rusted set of keys and disappeared back down the stairwell. Tentatively she walked further into her new apartment. The air smelled of sweat and moldy cheese. She considered opening a window but wasn't sure the stench of the street outside would fare any better.

Sighing deeply, she thought of her grandmother's house, of her white picket fence and small, immaculate lawn where Elise would sit and strum her guitar and bask in the sun. So far, New York was far from the dream she'd hoped it to be.

***

"You're going to need a job," Gloria, one of Elise's two roommates, declared fervently. She had arrived back at the apartment just over an hour ago wearing a bright red dress and matching apron. Gloria was an aspiring actress and had been living in the city for eighteen months.

"I was hoping I could earn with my music," Elise pointed at her guitar case which was now resting against the sofa.

"Nah, not going to happen," Gloria pointed a long purple nail at Elise and pursed her lips and shook her head quickly.

"You need real money and you need it now. You might be Taylor freaking Swift on that thing but getting noticed takes time. Until then, you got rent to pay."

Elise glanced despondently at her new acquaintance. She had hoped that moving to New York would mean escaping her old life; her old dead-end job, too, instead of just acquiring a new one.

"They're hiring at the café where I work," Gloria suggested helpfully. "Just waitressing, but the tips are good. I can put in a word for you if you like?"

"Yes, please, that'd be good," Elise smiled kindly, tucking a stray bang behind her ear.

"You're one of those Southern shy types," Gloria grinned, revealing two rows of immaculately white teeth.

"I give it three weeks and the city will have knocked that out of you!"

"You think?"

"City living is hard, country girl! Hope you're ready for it!"

***

Elise was halfway through her second shift at Deena's Diner and she was already exhausted. Her hair stuck to her head in clumps, soaked with sweat as she hurried among the tables to take the breakfast orders of the gathered regulars. Everyone had such specific needs:

"Fried eggs, but only one over easy."

"Coffee, just a dash of sugar and cream, not milk."

"French toast, but no syrup."

Elise frantically scribbled down everything she could and then dashed off into the intense heat of the kitchen to give the orders to Laurence, the resident chef. He was a big man who barked orders with ease and seemed to like giving the waitresses a hard time.

"His bark is worse than his bite," Gloria had whispered to Elise during her first shift. "You'll get used to everything, don't worry."

"I don't think your new girl can hack it!" Laurence had roared, laughing slightly as Elise, flustered, handed him a wad of new orders.

"She can handle it," Gloria confidently told the chef. "She's the next Claire Parry, don't you know?"

"Argh," Laurence waved a dismissive hand towards her. "Everyone is the next something or other. Why can't anyone just be new?"

"You're too cool, Laurence, you know that?" Gloria had teased him.

"Serve this up and stop wasting my time," Laurence had snapped back though his eyes were kind even if his tone wasn't.

Elise watched their back-and-forth banter with fear. She wasn't sure she'd ever be confident enough to talk back to Laurence like that. Heck, she couldn't talk back to anyone. Manners mattered, her grandmother was always telling her.

"Come on, move it!" a waitress nudged Elise sharply as she passed her by carrying a tray piled high with fresh dishes.

Gloria was off during Elise's second day at work. Apparently she had a casting call which she just couldn't miss. Elise felt a little lost without her new friend there to guide her. She did her best to keep on top of her orders, to remember the shorthand when she wrote things down, to take the correct order to the correct table, but after four hours her mind had turned to mush and her legs ached to the point where she feared they might just fall off.

Her time in the offices of Curtis Cleaning Products hadn't prepared her for the demands of such a physical job.

"Can I take your order?" she asked a little breathlessly as she approached her next table. A group of guys around her own age were settled within the booth. They were all handsome but the guy closest to her really stood out. He had jet-black hair cut in a trendy style and piercing blue eyes which were now observing Elise. She felt her cheeks beginning to burn.

"We'll have the usual," the blue-eyed stranger told her.

"The usual?" Elise reiterated in confusion. "I'm sorry, I'm new, I don't know what the usual is."

"Don't apologize," the stranger told her. "You've done nothing wrong, why are you apologizing?"

"I'm sorry–" Elise was getting flustered. What was the usual? Gloria hadn't mentioned that.

"Dylan, lay off her!" one of the other guys shouted, kicking his friend beneath the table.

"Yeah, man, she's new, give her a break," said another guy in the group.

So the handsome stranger had a name: Dylan.

"Four coffees, black, and four plates stacked as high as possible with pancakes," Dylan arched an eyebrow at her as he reeled off their usual order.

Elise scribbled furiously in the notepad she was clutching.

"Coming right up," she told them nervously.

"There's a big tip in it for you if it's in the next ten minutes or so," Dylan told her cockily, as though he had all the money in the world.

"We've got band practice at ten."

Band practice? Elise looked back at the group with renewed interest. Were they actually some big-shot band? There must be loads of famous bands living in

New York, was one of them there, right now, in the diner where she worked?

"I'm actually a musician," Elise told Dylan shyly, her eyes sparkling with excitement.

"No," Dylan shook his head and stared blankly at her. "You're a waitress who is about to lose out on my very generous tip."

Elise practically sprinted away from the table. She felt so humiliated. When she returned with their food fifteen minutes later, she deliberately stalled for as long as she could, and she refused to even look Dylan in the eye. She silently placed down their coffee and pancakes and left. As she walked away she was certain she could hear them all sniggering, probably about her. Whatever band they were in, she sure as hell wasn't going to listen to any of their songs.

The diner began to empty around ten. Elise watched Dylan and his band mates leave from a safe distance. They each wore skinny jeans and a statement t-shirts but Dylan also wore a leather jacket.

"He thinks he's so cool," Elise seethed to herself. When she was quite sure they were gone she went over to clear their table. They had left her a five-dollar tip, beside which was a hastily scribbled note:

"It could have been ten ;)." In protest she left the five dollars for someone else to claim.

A Dream for Two

At four o'clock Elise finished her shift, having endured the breakfast and lunch rush. At least she was free from doing the dinner shift. In contrast, Gloria was just about to start her shift. The girls passed on the street and briefly embraced before going their separate ways.

Elise's feet were now numb, having gone past the point of agony several hours ago. She walked briskly towards the subway entrance, careful to keep her purse pressed tightly against her body. She'd heard about the crime in New York and other cities and she refused to become a statistic. Besides, she could just imagine her grandmother's outrage if she got mugged. The old woman would be taking the next bus out there to hunt down the perpetrator herself.

As busy as the streets were, Elise tried to take in the city. She walked by diners, bookstores, souvenir shops, laundromats. The city seemed to have everything. She slowed when she approached a bar which was currently closed. On the window musical notes had been ornately painted and as she peered into the dark interior she could make out the outline of a grand piano.

Eagle's Bar, the sign read. Elise continued to survey the exterior of the bar. A worn cocktail menu was plastered up outside and beside that a poster, much

19

brighter and newer, advertised a weekly open mic night. The next one was the coming Thursday. Elise mentally ran through her work schedule. She was on early starts all week.

"Walk-Ins Welcome" was written on the poster.

There was apparently no need to sign up for the open mic night. Elise continued to look at the poster. It boasted of an eager, live audience willing to find New York's next big voice in music.

"No, you're a waitress," Dylan the band idiot's voice bounced around Elise's head. She swatted at it as though it were an unwanted bug. She'd prove him wrong. She'd go to the open mic night that Thursday, play her music and have people appreciate her for being a musician. She was so much more than a waitress, than an office worker. Her grandmother had helped her see that, had helped her find her previously lost faith in herself.

"Hey, watch it!" someone declared tersely, almost colliding with Elise as she stood motionless on the sidewalk reading the poster.

"Sorry," Elise instinctively responded in her soft Southern lilt. Then she internally berated herself. She really did need to stop apologizing so much.

Chapter 3

Thursday arrived faster than Elise would have liked. That morning as she worked her shift in the diner she couldn't stop thinking about her upcoming performance. She'd never attended an open mic night before and had no idea what to expect. She wondered how polished the other performers would be, how kind the audience were. All these thoughts rattled around her head as she dutifully poured coffee and took what felt like countless breakfast orders.

"It's a what, now?" Annabelle asked in her prolonged drawl. Elise was propped up against a wall in the alley behind the diner, calling her grandmother during her break.

"An open mic night," Elise repeated.

"What does that do?"

"I'm not entirely sure," Elise admitted. "But I guess you go up on stage and sing some of your songs before a live audience."

"Ooh, I wish I could be there."

"Me too," Elise smiled sadly.

"Have you decided what you're going to sing?"

"Um…" Elise hadn't given much thought to which song she'd actually perform, she'd spent too long worrying about how the event would unfold and how many people would be there.

"I love 'Where the River Parts,'" her grandmother suggested helpfully. It was a bittersweet song Elise had penned when she was a teenager about loss and moving forward.

"Do you think?" Elise frowned and moved her cell phone to her other ear as her arm was growing numb.

"You don't think that song is too sad?"

"No!" her grandmother exclaimed dramatically. "It is a beautiful song, honey. You always perform it so beautifully too."

"Okay, I'll go with that then." Elise felt a little better to have a plan formulating with regards to her performance.

"Break a leg, isn't that what they say in the business?"

"I think that's in theater, but thanks."

Elise ended the call and shoved her phone back into her jeans pocket before heading back into the heat of the kitchen. She had a slight spring in her step as she walked. As nervous as she was about the open mic night, she was excited to share her music with the world. No one other than her grandmother had ever even heard "Where the River Parts." In a few hours, new sets of ears would hear it and Elise was giddy with both nerves and excitement at the prospect.

***

"You look great," Gloria took a moment to give Elise's outfit her seal of approval before she headed out to work.

"Do you think?" Elise looked down at her skinny jeans and pink vest top. She had worried that she'd look too casual but she wasn't really sure what she should wear to an open mic night.

"You look casual yet stylish," Gloria grinned. She was still wearing her bright red uniform.

"Thanks."

"Want me to walk there with you?" Gloria offered, eyeing the large guitar case resting by the front door to the apartment. Elise was tiny in stature and almost dwarfed by it.

"I'll be okay."

"You sure?" Gloria frowned at the case. "That thing looks like it weighs more than you!"

"I'm used to carrying it around," Elise blushed. She actually found hauling around the weight of her guitar case oddly comforting. Feeling its immense weight against her back as she moved made her feel less alone, almost like she was protected by armor.

"Okay. Promise to text me how tonight goes?"

"I promise," Elise nodded sincerely.

"And remember," Gloria placed her hands upon her friend's slim shoulders, "when you get up, you're singing only for you, don't go forgetting that."

"I won't."

***

People were already milling around on the street outside Eagle's Bar when Elise approached with her guitar strapped to her back. Even though it was now dark she'd hadn't felt any apprehensions as she boarded the subway alone. She felt safe with her guitar.

Everyone outside the bar was dressed in a trendy yet casual style. Some of them were smoking, some were just talking. A few pairs of interested eyes looked up as Elise walked by but no one said anything.

Inside the bar was dimly lit. There was a main room, filled with two-seater tables on which candles burned. On the right-hand wall there was a bar seemingly offering every drink imaginable. Elise briefly scanned the rows of liquor bottles, amazed that so many different types of alcohol even existed. Then at the far end of the room was the raised platform which was the stage. On it there was a solitary chair behind a microphone on a stand. It was so stripped back, so exposed. Elise suddenly felt sick. For a brief moment she considered running back into the dark of the New York night when a hand gripped her shoulder and spun her around.

"You here for open mic night?" a bearded man seemingly in his late thirties asked. He had a diamond earring which sparkled within his earlobe.

"Umm…" Elise felt the weight of her guitar against her. It was blaringly obvious that she was there to perform.

"Yes," she sounded as timid as a mouse as she squeaked her response.

"Okay, sign up here." The guy handed her a clipboard upon which half a dozen names had already been written down.

"If you want to throw up, the restrooms are over there," he pointed to the left side of the bar.

"I'm fine," Elise confirmed as she scrawled her name with a shaking hand.

"Take a seat and we'll give you a shout when it's your turn. Also, you might want a drink, take the edge off."

Elise wasn't a big drinker but she had to admit that she did need something to take the edge off. She nervously headed over to the bar where six or seven people were already standing. She ordered a neat vodka. She knew it would burn as she knocked it back but she also knew that it should be enough to dampen any of her nerves. She took a second shot of vodka over to a table with her and settled down towards the back of the room.

As it drew closer to the opening act starting, more and more people began to filter into the bar. Soon almost all of the tables were occupied and the whole room buzzed with excited energy. People were talking among themselves but Elise was sitting alone with just her guitar for company.

"Okay, let's get things going." The guy who had handed her the clipboard came out onto the stage and a hush fell over the crowd. A crude spotlight was directed onto him which he seemed oblivious of. He leaned forward and spoke directly into the microphone:

"Thanks for coming out to Eagle's Bar tonight, we appreciate your support, and money well spent at the bar."

Laughter rippled through the crowd.

"We always have some real talent up on this stage and this Thursday night is no exception. And so, to kick us off is one of our regulars. Let's give it up for Dylan Cornish."

The crowd applauded vigorously, some people even cheered as the clipboard guy was replaced by the first act. Elise couldn't quite believe her eyes when he stepped up to the microphone. Dylan Cornish was the same Dylan from the diner, the same guy who had labeled her just a waitress. Anger made Elise's body tighten.

"Evening all," he spoke confidently into the microphone and some women in the crowd wolf whistled at him.

"This is just a little number I'm working on," he explained as someone near the front of the stage handed up to him a large keyboard on a stand. He carefully placed it in front of him, drew the microphone close and then lowered his hand to the digital keys.

Elise watched in shocked awe as Dylan Cornish performed two beautiful songs. His voice oozed emotion and had a rustic quality but his melodies were upbeat and infuriatingly catchy. He sung about the frustrations of being employed and in his second song, the beauty of making love to a girl you'd been crushing on. The second song made Elise blush. When he was finished the crowd erupted into applause. Dylan Cornish was clearly a hit but evidently he wasn't quite as big a star as Elise had originally believed. After all, he was here at the same bar as her trying to catch the same break.

As Dylan confidently sauntered off the stage Elise sank down in her seat so that he wouldn't see her. She realized how foolish that was considering that she'd soon be up on stage and then of course he'd see her. But she wanted to avoid facing him for as long as possible.

Four performers and an additional shot of neat vodka later, Elise's name was called. Taking a deep breath she picked up her guitar and approached the stage.

"Elise here is a newcomer," clipboard guy explained to the crowd. "So go easy on her."

"You need to hurl, sweetheart?" someone kindly heckled. Elise ignored them. The walk towards the stage felt like the green mile but she kept her head down and remained focused. Her hands wanted to shake as she set her case down and popped it open but she refused to let them.

She sat down on the chair, and clipboard guy lowered the microphone to her level as she was the shortest performer that night by far. She placed the guitar strap around her neck and the spotlight was directed at her. It was so bright that it blocked out the crowd. If Dylan had spotted her by now, she thankfully couldn't see his reaction.

An anticipated hush fell over the crowd. Elise positioned her fingers upon the strings. She closed her eyes and reminded herself of all the times she'd played this song, all the times she'd strummed the music, sung the lyrics. She didn't even remember to introduce the song, she just played.

Elise played as though she was sitting in her grandmother's garden, beneath the willow tree with no one there listening. She was alone with just her music. She sang "Where the River Parts." At times her voice cracked with pain but it always retained its sweet, strong pitch. She strummed the final chord and held her breath. Silence.

Her heart began to hammer against her chest. Had she been so truly awful that the crowd couldn't even bring themselves to applaud? Surely they'd applaud her out of politeness, or even pity. And then all of a sudden the silence was shattered. People applauded and cheered as emphatically as they had after Dylan's set. Elise beamed with surprised joy as she carefully stood up, picked up her guitar case and left the stage.

"That was actually okay," a familiar voice declared loudly as she neared the sanctuary of her table at the back. Dylan was casually leaning against the wall. He turned away from the stage to look at her.

"Just okay?" Elise asked. Buoyed by her performance, she felt invincible. She wasn't about to let some cocky guy bring her down, no matter how handsome he was. And he did look handsome. He had on his usual leather jacket and dirtied jeans with work boots. His blue eyes regarded Elise with interest and he raised a hand to move some of his dark hair out of his line of sight.

"You should take okay," Dylan pointed at her, smiling wryly. "Okay is decent, especially for a waitress."

Elise narrowed her eyes at him, willing herself to remain composed.

"I told you, I'm a musician."

"So if I head to Deena's Diner tomorrow you won't be there serving coffee?" Dylan raised an eyebrow at her.

"You're one to talk!" Elise fired at him. "You act like you're some big hotshot musician but you're not! Anyway, I thought you were in a band?"

"I am," Dylan stared intently at her. "But this here, it's just for me." Then he gave her a quick wink, stood up and walked away.

Chapter 4

Elise couldn't stop thinking about Dylan throughout the following week. There was something about his music, or rather the way he sang it, which was just so alluring. He had totally gotten under her skin. But then she hated how arrogant he was. He'd called her just a waitress? Who did he think he was?

"He sounds like a bad boy," Gloria purred with approval over lunch the following Saturday.

"He's just a pain," Elise shrugged. "I just wish he hadn't been so rude to me."

"I like his style, treat them mean, keep them keen," Gloria gave her friend a cheeky wink.

"I'm not keen," Elise insisted. "And he's just mean."

"So you're not going to the next open mic night?"

"No, I'm going," Elise nodded as she cut up her waffle which had been drowned in maple syrup.

Gloria arched an eyebrow in judgment.

"I'm going because it's good for me!" Elise clarified. "It's a chance for me to perform my music to a live audience. Plus I might get spotted by someone important!"

"Someone like Dylan?" Gloria teased.

"No," Elise could feel her cheeks reddening. "Someone like a talent scout, or a music producer."

"New York is full of open mic nights, you know," Gloria mused. "You could just try your hand somewhere else, somewhere Dylan-free."

Elise chewed on a mouthful of sweet waffle and realized that her friend was right. She could go somewhere else but she didn't want to. As much as she hated to admit it, she was hoping she'd get to see Dylan again. Or at least see him perform again. When he played she felt the marrow in her bones melt. He was so effortlessly sexy, so cool, calm and serene yet he also seemed impossibly powerful. He was such a heady mix of extremes. Each time Elise banished him from her thoughts he popped up again, more brooding and mysterious than the time before.

He'd yet to return to Deena's Diner. Elise felt her heart sink each morning he didn't show. Was he avoiding her? She hoped not. But then he had only been rude to her. He was arrogant and pigheaded and if he didn't show up at the diner again he'd be doing her a favor.

"Oh, you got it bad!" Gloria pointed her fork across the table at Elise.

"Huh?"

"You keep getting that dreamy look all girls get when they meet their Prince Charming."

"Please," Elise tried to sound dismissive. "Dylan is no Prince Charming."

"Then wipe that dreamy look off your face!"

Elise rolled her eyes and tried to avoid admitting that she couldn't wipe the look off her face any more than she could wipe Dylan out of her mind. It was as if he'd set up roost within her thoughts as he was constantly there, taunting her, mocking her. She feared that if she didn't stop thinking about Dylan Cornish soon she'd go crazy!

***

Elise barely slept the night before the next open mic night. She kept going over her set in her mind and she kept rehearsing what she'd say to Dylan if she saw him. It drove her crazy the way he kept saying she was just a waitress. He was in the same situation as her, why wasn't he being more supportive of a fellow struggling musician?

With her guitar on her back Elise headed back to Eagle's Bar. This time when she entered the clipboard guy quickly approached her before she'd had chance to place her heavy case down.

"Are you playing tonight?" he asked her a little too eagerly.

"Yeah," Elise replied politely.

"Great, because you killed it last time," he smiled. "Good for you." He handed her the clipboard and she neatly wrote down her name. Her heart almost stopped when she spotted the name messily scrawled before it:

Dylan Cornish.

"It should be a good turnout tonight," clipboard guy declared before heading off to jot down more names.

"It's always a good turnout when I'm here." Elise didn't need to turn around to see who had spoken but she did anyway. Dylan had sat down on a nearby table, his legs propped up on a chair, leaning back casually as though he owned the place. In his hand he held a glass of what appeared to be neat vodka.

"You're so modest," Elise told him sourly. She picked up her case and prepared to move when Dylan promptly lowered his feet and kicked the now spare chair towards her.

"What's the rush, waitress? Sit down, take a load off."

"My name is Elise," she corrected him as she lowered herself down into the seat despite her reservations. Somehow she just couldn't resist him.

"So you came back for round two." Dylan smiled at her before knocking back the contents of his glass.

Elise wasn't sure if he was talking about the open mic night or himself.

"I enjoyed performing," Elise admitted.

"Everyone always does," Dylan declared grandly.

"At least I do it for the music rather than the adoration."

Dylan pointed a finger at himself and made a jovial expression.

"You think I do it for adoration?"

"Of course."

"You think I just do it to meet chicks?"

"Don't you?" Elise challenged.

"What's it matter to you? Seems you've already made your mind up on me." Dylan shrugged, suddenly seeming bored by their conversation.

"You keep calling me a waitress! You won't stop judging me!" Elise was about to launch into a tirade at him when Dylan was called up on to the stage against his usual round of applause.

Just like the week before he was amazing. He sung with soul and connected to his music in a way Elise hadn't seen before. As she watched him she became transfixed by his melody, by the way his strong hands effortlessly navigated their way across the keyboard.

She was so swept away by his music that she didn't realize he'd been staring directly at her the whole time he'd been performing. As their eyes locked she felt herself turning crimson. When everyone else was applauding his performance Elise was lowering herself self-consciously into her seat. Why had he been watching her the whole time? Was he trying to prove a point?

Before he could return to the table and explain himself, Elise was called up to the stage.

Her second performance felt easier than her first one. Again she imagined she was back home beneath the willow tree, singing away her sadness on a hot summer afternoon. At the end everyone applauded, and one overzealous member of the audience even whooped. She was feeling good as she headed back out into the bar. She braced herself for whatever remark Dylan was undoubtedly going to give her but to her dismay he didn't reappear. As Elise sat down to watch the rest of the performers she felt her good mood begin to evaporate. Dylan Cornish had left.

***

Elise was still feeling blue over Dylan's premature departure at the open mic night as she hustled around the breakfast tables. Her shift had felt unbearably long as she tended to a stream of patrons. At least she was finding things easier at the diner. She was faster taking orders and had even started to anticipate what some regulars would want. As a result, her tips were becoming more generous.

It was late morning and the breakfast crowd had thinned out when Elise headed over to a recently occupied booth in her area. A guy was sitting alone. His back was to her so she could only see the intense collection of dark hair which covered his head.

"What can I get you?" Elise asked sweetly as she approached him. She always made her Southern accent as thick as possible when working as people seemed to love it and tip more generously when they heard it.

"Ah, so still a waitress then?" Dylan Cornish looked up at her with his brilliant blue eyes and Elise felt the fake smile fall from her lips.

"I'll have a coffee, black, and some pancakes."

"What are you doing here?" Elise demanded rudely, momentarily forgetting herself.

"Ordering a late breakfast," Dylan shrugged. "Is that a problem?"

Elise frowned at him. Had he even stayed to hear her sing last night? She wished she didn't care as much as she did. She took his order and stormed off towards the kitchen.

Ten minutes later she returned to his table to pour his coffee. She'd been putting it off for as long as she could but knew she'd get in trouble if his mug remained empty any longer. She refused to make eye contact with him as she poured the dark caffeinated liquid.

"I liked your set last night," Dylan told her kindly. "Your song makes me sad in a way I've not known before."

Surprised, Elise looked down at him. His eyes were wide and his mouth was drawn in a thin line. He didn't seem to be hiding behind his usual cocky bravado. When she looked at him he continued.

"Like, it made me sad but wistful. Normally songs just do one or the other."

"Thanks," Elise told him sincerely.

"I acknowledge good music when I hear it," Dylan smiled softly.

"Then why do you keep calling me a waitress?" Elise challenged.

"Because you are one," Dylan replied flatly. For a moment Elise feared he was just going to be a jerk to her again.

"And because you don't like it," he added. He self-consciously ran a hand through his hair and actually looked nervous. Elise thought she must be seeing things.

"When I call you a waitress, it reminds you why you're here, it ignites that fire of ambition in you, does it not? When I say it, you're desperate to prove me wrong?"

Elise nodded slowly, knowing he was right.

"You've got potential," he told her, his eyes sparkling. "I'd hate to see you waste it so I'm just trying to help keep that fire burning."

"Why did you run out after my performance?" Elise blurted. She was desperate to know. She's spent all night concocting theories in her mind. Her favorite was that he was actually living a double life as a superhero and had left to put on his cape and go restore justice to the city.

"You think I'm a sleaze," Dylan shrugged casually.

"No, I don't," Elise blushed.

"Then go out for a drink with me," Dylan smiled warmly.

"Are you asking me out?" Elise was completely caught off guard.

"Or don't," Dylan leaned back in the booth. He was wearing his leather jacket. "I'm not the guy you think I am. I play because I love the music, the adoration is just a bonus," he smirked playfully.

"But I'd like you to see the real me, the me who burns, just as you do, to succeed."

"Okay, let's go for drinks," Elise tried to sound nonchalant even though she was shaking. She was terrified that she was going to drop the coffeepot she was holding. She just hoped that Dylan couldn't see her trembling.

"Sounds good," Dylan ran a hand through his hair again.

"Where are your band mates today?" Elise changed the subject to try to ease her mounting nerves.

"Probably still in bed," Dylan scorned his absent friends. He seemed displeased. "Let's just say that they lack my commitment to the music. They definitely are in it for the adoration."

"I'm sorry."

"Don't be," Dylan shook his head and some of his dark hair fell into his eyes which made him look devastatingly sexy.

"I'm just tired of holding the band together. I guess that's why I like to perform on my own sometimes."

"But sometimes I find it so terrifying to be up there alone, laying it bare for everyone to see," Elise confessed.

"Laying it bare? Whoa!" Dylan raised his hands and grinned at her. "We're not even on our date yet, try to hold yourself back!"

Elise rolled her eyes and laughed at his cheeky comment. Some of his bravado was leaking back into him so she sidled back to the kitchen to collect his order. She liked the stripped-back version of Dylan Cornish she'd just met and she hoped that she'd get to see more of him.

Chapter 5

"So, are you bringing it tonight?" Dylan asked from where he was leaning against the wall of Eagle's Bar in his leather jacket, his arms folded across his chest.

"Bringing what?" Elise asked as she dropped down her guitar case and sighed gratefully to be relieved of its weight.

"You know, it?" Dylan grinned. "The thing that makes the crowd go crazy, the thing that makes people buy your record or go to your show!"

"Oh, it," Elise smiled at him mockingly. "I bring it every time I perform, thank you very much."

"Maybe," Dylan tilted his head in approval. "But do you bring enough of it? Each night, I draw the biggest applause in this place."

"Is that so?"

Elise tried to conceal how delighted she was not only that he was there but that he was talking to her. Since their encounter in the diner she felt like she knew him better than she did before.

"How about we make a bet?" Dylan suggested, his blue eyes sparkling mischievously.

"What sort of bet?" Elise asked, intrigued.

"Whoever gets the biggest applause buys the drinks."

"What drinks?"

"At our date," Dylan stated factually. "I figured we could go out after tonight. I like to stay out after I've performed because I always get such a buzz from being on stage and don't want to come down."

Elise knew exactly how he felt. Being on stage, performing to a live crowd was utterly intoxicating. Each time she finished playing she was almost trembling with excitement. She'd never felt anything quite like it.

"Okay," Elise lifted her chin confidently. "It's a bet."

"Ooh, game on!" Dylan smiled, clearly elated by the prospect of competition. "You better hope you brought it!"

He winked at her and then sauntered over to the bar to order himself a couple of shots before his performance.

***

Dylan's set was before hers and as usual he received rapturous applause when he finished. The audience really did love him. Elise wondered what he was like when he performed with his band. He rarely spoke about them. Perhaps they were a much different style than his solo music. She was interested to find out. She kept thinking of things to say to him during their date. Her biggest fear was that she'd struggle to keep the conversation going and that he'd find her boring. She could ask him about his band. She made a mental note to do just that.

When the clipboard guy called Elise's name she felt fired up to perform. Some people even applauded her as she made her way to the stage. She'd been in New York less than a month and this was already her third open mic night. She knew that her grandmother would be impressed by those numbers. She'd say that Elise was "taking the bull by the horns" and being the master of her own destiny.

But when Elise sat down on the stage she had to silence all the voices in her mind and concentrate only on her music. She had to return to the heat of her grandmother's backyard, imagine the wind rustling through the long, hanging leaves of the willow tree and then she'd lift her hand to her guitar and play.

As she finished the gathered crowd broke out into thunderous applause. When Elise gazed out at their unfamiliar faces she realized that more and more people were coming each week. Some people were standing at the back, unable to find a seat. She smiled modestly at their applause, tucked her guitar back into its case and dropped down from the stage. Dylan quickly found her. He came and stood beside her. He smelled of liquor and cologne. The cheap kind that you buy in the supermarket but it smelled good on him.

"So, do you think you topped me?" he asked.

"I'm not sure," Elise admitted. It was hard to judge who had received the more rapturous applause. As they walked through the dense crowd Dylan placed his hand on Elise's lower back to guide her. Her whole body tingled at his touch and she felt her cheeks flush. He was so handsome she found it hard to focus when she was around him.

"I think you edged me out," Dylan leaned down and whispered the words directly into her ear, his hot breath fluttering against her cheek. "How about we go out for that drink now?"

Elise nodded, careful not to seem too eager, as Dylan guided her out of the heaving bar.

They walked down towards a quieter venue, a bar called Oscar's which served exotically named cocktails.

"Since I'm buying I insist you buy something with an overly elaborate name," Dylan instructed as they stood at the bar.

Nervously Elise tucked her bangs behind her ear and perused the menu. All of the names sound elaborate to her.

"How about a Singapore Sling?" she wondered, noticing that the cocktail was pink which appealed to her.

"Great," Dylan grinned. Then he gestured to the barman, "We'll take two, please."

"It's a pink drink, you know," Elise laughed as they went and sat at their table.

"I'm comfortable enough in my manliness to drink pink," Dylan quipped.

***

Three cocktails later and Elise was certain that she'd never laughed so much in her life. Her cheeks ached from the constant bouts of giggles Dylan sent her into. He was so quick-witted and funny, and worldly. He'd traveled all across Europe and America with only a backpack. He seemed to have had an endless stream of adventures. Elise's life felt unbearably dull by comparison.

"You must have been somewhere," Dylan pressed her.

"I've been to New York," Elise shrugged lightly as she sipped the last of her third cocktail. She felt as if she'd just passed tipsy and was heading towards drunk.

"So you've never been on vacation?"

"Nope," Elise shook her head. "My grandmother couldn't afford it."

"What about your folks?"

Elise stiffened. She was lucid enough to know it would be a mistake to reveal too much to Dylan too soon. She didn't want him thinking she was this sad case from the South with nothing but a sob story and a guitar. She wanted to be interesting and well-traveled like him, not just tragic.

"Umm," Elise spun her straw around in her glass, playing for time. She didn't want to lie to him but she wasn't sure that full-on honesty was the right tack either.

"Hey, you don't have to tell me," Dylan sounded casual but she saw the hurt look briefly flash across his handsome face. He thought she was deliberating holding back from him, which she was.

"Look, if I tell you, you're not allowed to see me any differently."

"Okay?" Dylan eyed her dubiously.

"And I'm only telling you because I'm pretty close to drunk and you're too cute to not tell."

"You think I'm cute?" Dylan lit up at this.

"You want to know or not?" The cocktails gave Elise enough bravado to not care that she'd just told him he was cute.

"I want to know," Dylan told her sincerely. He reached out and placed his hands over hers. He felt so warm.

"My folks died when I was young. They gave me my first guitar. I've lived with my grandmother ever since."

Dylan looked at her intently and squeezed her hands.

"I'm sorry, but I do see you differently now," he apologized gently. Elise felt her cheeks heating up, tears threatening to come cascading down them. He didn't like her anymore. She knew she shouldn't have said anything, it was too soon to dump all her baggage on him.

"Before you seemed like this delicate Southern flower. But now I see I was wrong. You're not a flower; you're a diamond. You're impossibly beautiful and rare but also amazingly strong."

Elise felt her eyes watering. It was easily the nicest thing anyone had ever said to her. She could feel her heart racing in her chest.

"Let's get out of here," Dylan suggested.

They walked hand in hand down the sidewalk towards the subway station. Elise's guitar case was now strapped to his back. In a gentlemanly gesture he'd insisted on carrying it and the Southern sensibility in Elise liked him for doing so.

Slowly they walked down beneath the city. The subway platform was eerily quiet at such a late hour. A few homeless people had sought shelter down there, bundling themselves up in all they had, hoping that they wouldn't be moved along and would be able to steal a few hour's rest.

Elise liked holding Dylan's hand. It made everything about the city seem more magical. It stopped being this huge, imposing place and became somewhere that needed to be explored.

"You know, you really annoyed me when I first met you," she declared drunkenly as they stopped on the platform. Dylan shrugged off the guitar case and dropped it by their feet. Soon they would be parting ways.

"Did I win you over though?" he asked, drawing close to her. Their noses were almost touching as Elise whispered in response:

"Yeah, I guess you did."

Dylan leaned down and touched his lips against hers. He felt surprisingly soft. He lowered his hands down her back and drew her into him. Tenderly the kiss deepened. Elise felt her heart begin to flutter madly as he pressed his tongue against hers. It was the most amazing kiss of her life. Her entire body melted against him as they kissed. She wanted the world to end right then, when she was locked in his embrace, connected with a kiss. She didn't want to have to walk away from Dylan Cornish, she didn't want the kiss to have to end. But the sound of the oncoming train made him pull away. Breathless, they looked deep into one another's eyes.

"I think this is you," Dylan eventually broke the silence, nodding in the direction of the train.

Elise reached down for her case but kept her eyes locked onto him.

"I don't want to go," she admitted.

"Then don't," Dylan drew her in for another kiss and Elise's guitar case dropped to the ground with a dull thud. She missed the next three trains which passed through the station but she was oblivious to their arrival. The kiss was all consuming. The world beyond it had suddenly ceased to exist.

But as midnight approached Elise knew the magic of the kiss was about to wear off.

"I really should get back," she said regretfully as she picked her case up for the second time. This time she took a step back, creating distance between them so that she wouldn't feel compelled to enter into another kiss.

"Thanks for a great night," Dylan told her sincerely.

"You too," she smiled warmly at him.

"You're my diamond," he told her, reaching forward to plant one final, soft kiss upon her lips.

"And I'm no fool. I know that once you find something as precious as a rare diamond, you don't ever let it go."

Fueled by his romantic words Elise floated over to the train. He remained standing on the platform, watching her leave. Leaning back in her seat Elise thought her heart might explode from all the happiness pumping through it. She'd never felt that way before. She felt giddy from the cocktails and from the kissing but she knew it was more than that. She'd heard people sing about it. She'd never felt it before, but somehow she knew that she was falling in love.

Chapter 6

Elise floated through the following week. Even her shifts at the diner became more bearable as at the end of them she'd get to see Dylan. He quickly integrated himself into her life. He'd meet her after work and walk her back to the apartment. They'd walk hand in hand, lost in their own little world. For Elise, New York had never seemed more beautiful. The streetlights glittered magically like stars and even the putrid smell of car exhausts seemed more comforting.

"Girl, you're in love," Gloria noted one morning over breakfast. It was a rare treat for the girls to both have the day off together. Elise had hoped that she'd get to spend the day with Dylan but he'd been called in for a last-minute band practice.

"They never want to practice," he'd told her over the phone the previous night. "So there must be something important coming up."

"So you can't miss it," Elise had nodded sadly as she sat cross-legged on the sofa.

"No, I can't miss it, I'm sorry," Dylan sighed. "But I'll see you tonight at Eagle's."

***

"I'm not in love," Elise blushed as she stuck her spoon into her bowl of cereal.

"You so are!" Gloria beamed. "It's written all across your face!"

"No, it's not!" Elise protested as the red of her cheeks deepened.

Gloria was giggling in delight to herself.

"Oooh, you're in love! What will your grandmother say?"

Elise paused, her spoonful of sugary cereal half way on its journey to her mouth. What would her grandmother say? She was certain that she wouldn't approve of Dylan. He was in a band and wore a leather jacket, hardly the poster child for decent boyfriends.

"Hey, don't go worrying about your Grams just yet," Gloria reached across the upturned crate they were using for a table and gripped her friend's hand.

"Just enjoy being with Dylan. New relationships are like the best thing ever. If I could bottle up that feeling and sell it I'd become a billionaire overnight."

***

And so Elise tried to just focus on her newfound love with Dylan. She found herself humming on the subway when she thought about it. She couldn't wait to see him at Eagle's Bar that night. The day had dragged without his presence to break it up. He was all she could think about.

Elise hauled her guitar on her back towards the bar and instinctively looked around for Dylan but he was nowhere to be seen. There were some familiar faces gathered there to listen to that night's performances but none of them were Dylan's. Elise began to feel dejected as she lowered herself into a vacant seat. Perhaps his band practice had gone on longer than he'd anticipated?

Dylan still hadn't showed when Elise's name was called. She pushed her shoulders back and forced herself to walk confidently towards the stage, promising herself that he'd be there soon, he'd probably arrive as she was singing.

Luckily Elise always lost herself in her music. As soon as she began to strum the familiar notes she was transported back to the South, back to her happy place. She sung the melody and smiled sweetly for the audience. As she concluded to rapturous applause she bowed modestly and clambered off the stage. Sitting back down at her table she nursed a fresh glass of cranberry juice. She no longer needed the hit of vodka to help her get up on stage. She was high on love.

"Hey, that was some performance."

Elise glanced up expectantly, hoping to see Dylan grinning down at her but she didn't recognize the smartly dressed man who sat down across from her.

He had short peroxide-blonde hair and wore a suit coupled with Converse shoes. He was unlike anyone else who had gathered at the bar, He had a professional aura which made him strange.

"Um, thanks," Elise replied politely, hoping that he wasn't coming on to her. She always found it awkward to rebuff a guy's advances.

"I mean really, it was exceptional."

"Thanks."

"I'm Jake Roberts," the blonde man extended his hand towards her and she reluctantly shook it.

"I work for Cloud Records."

Elise blinked at him in shock. Cloud Records was the biggest label around, having people like Claire Parry and Ted Steerman on its books.

"I heard about you through the grapevine as it were," Jake continued. "I thought I'd come out here and check you out and I certainly wasn't disappointed." He reached into his jacket and pulled out a crisp white business card which he slid across to Elise.

"You're exactly the sort of sound the label has been looking for. You're young, fresh but also with depth.

I'd love it if you could give the office a call and we can arrange a time for you to come in and discuss things in more detail."

"What would we discuss?" Elise was still struggling to understand what was happening.

"We'd love to make a record with you," Jake grinned. He was a strange mixture of both genuine emotion and salesmanship and Elise was still unsure if she should trust him.

"Are you…is this…for real?" Elise picked up the business card and frowned at it. The card was extremely stylish with Jake's name, job title and contact details embossed on it beneath the iconic Cloud Records logo.

"It's most definitely for real," Jake reassured her. "Give me a call tomorrow. And whatever sucky job you're currently spilling your guts out for, quit it."

Elise's mouth was still hanging open as Jake stood up and walked away.

The rest of the night went by in a blur. Elise watched the remaining acts but she wasn't really interested in their performance. She just wanted to get back to the apartment and call Dylan. But he had promised to meet her at Eagle's Bar so she felt compelled to see out the rest of the night in the hope that he might show up. As the last performer exited the stage her persistence paid off.

The gathered crowd was thinning as Dylan sauntered in. He smiled as soon as he saw Elise and quickly came and sat beside her. He tenderly kissed her on the lips before saying anything.

"I'm sorry I'm so late," he apologized sincerely. "I got held up at band practice."

"It's okay."

"And I've actually got something to tell you."

"Me too!" Elise gushed. Now that Dylan was there everything immediately felt better and her chest swelled with joyous excitement.

"You first," Dylan prompted her. Elise showed him Jake's business card. Dylan observed it with interest and nodded slowly.

"That's…awesome," he finally enthused. "Cloud Records is huge, Elise. They'll make you a star."

"You think?" Elise asked excitedly.

"Well, I think you're already a star," Dylan gently tucked some of her hair back behind her ear. "But Cloud Records will just help the rest of the world see what I see and fall in love with you."

Elise felt her heart stop in her chest. Was he saying that he loved her? They still had yet to utter those three small words of infinite power to one another. She was about to press him on it when he decided to tell her his news.

"The reason I got called into band practice today was because we've actually just been signed."

"What? Are you serious?" Elise's dark eyes grew wide with interest.

"As a heart attack," Dylan nodded. "We are now signed with Epic Albums."

"Wow, Dylan, that's amazing!"

"Yeah," Dylan smiled but he didn't seem overly enthused by his own amazing news.

"I can't believe we've both basically been signed on the same day!"

"It's a strange world," Dylan interlocked Elise's hand with his own. "But we can't let this change anything," he told her sincerely.

"What would it change?" Elise asked, concerned.

"I don't know," Dylan admitted. "But we are still so new. I don't want anything to come along and derail us."

"It won't," Elise promised him, planting a tender kiss upon his lips. "Nothing can come between us."

A Dream for Two

***

Elise shivered slightly on the stoop which led up to her apartment building. Dylan was beside her, holding her guitar case. She wanted to invite him in but there were already two people sleeping in there, it would hardly be private.

"I have like, the most populated apartment in New York," she explained.

"It's okay," Dylan placed the guitar case by his feet so that he could wrap his arms around her. "I can wait."

She leaned into his chest and savored his scent. He smelled of cologne, cinnamon and ambition.

"I'm glad your band got signed," she mumbled dreamily into his chest.

"I'm glad you got signed." He lifted her chin and tilted her face up towards his. They kissed and it was deep and passionate and turned Elise's legs to jelly.

"God, I wish you could come up," she whispered when they eventually parted.

"Me too," Dylan agreed, resting his forehead against hers. The night was so cool that their breath was misting before them.

"You should get inside, it's cold," he told her sadly.

"You keep me warm," Elise smiled coyly.

They kissed again, for even longer this time.

"You're a tough woman to walk away from," Dylan sighed, still holding her tight.

"Dylan?"

"Yeah?"

"No matter what happens with our record deals, know that nothing will change between us."

"I hope not."

"It won't!" Elise insisted. "I know it won't."

"How do you know that?"

"Because I love you." The words slid easily off Elise's tongue. She loved how they sounded now that she had breathed life into them. She did love him. She'd loved him since their first kiss.

"I love you too," Dylan replied sincerely, stroking her cheek tenderly.

"Aww, you two are so cute!" a voice chortled from above them.

Blushing, Elise looked up as Dylan's grip tightened protectively around her. Gloria was hanging out of their apartment building, smiling broadly at them.

"Hurry up and get your ass up here!" she playfully ordered Elise. "I've been waiting forever for you to get in and debrief me on your night!"

"Duty calls, I suppose," Elise joked. Dylan kissed her softly on the lips.

"Come on!" Gloria insisted. "I'm freezing my ass off with this window open!"

"Nice to meet you," Dylan waved up at her as Elise began to ascend the final few steps of the stoop.

"You too!" Gloria waved at him. Then she averted her gaze to Elise. "Oh my God, he is totally hot. I can see why you're crushing on him so hard!"

"I'm right here!" Dylan pointed at himself and smiled.

"Do you have any brothers?" Gloria called to him. "Older or younger, I'm not picky!"

"Sorry, no brothers."

"Cousins?" Gloria asked hopefully. Dylan laughed and waved as he sauntered down onto the sidewalk.

"I'll see you tomorrow," he told Elise, holding her intensely in his gaze.

"Yeah," Elise had to prop herself up against the door as her legs were still jellified from his kiss.

"Tomorrow." She instantly hated tomorrow for being an entire day away, it already felt like an eternity.

"Make sure you call Jake," Dylan reminded her. "Sometimes opportunity only knocks once, you don't want to miss it."

"I'll call." Elise unlocked her front door and entered her apartment building. She realized with a shiver that it was just as cold inside as it was outside. But she didn't care. She sighed wistfully as she leaned back against the door. The interest from Cloud Records was great but it paled in comparison to Dylan's declaration of love. When Elise fell asleep, she was thinking solely about him, not even sparing a thought for the meteoric deal she was about to strike with one of the country's biggest music labels.

Chapter 7

"I hope you don't enjoy daylight," Jake quipped as Elise handed the signed contract back to him.

"Daylight?" She furrowed her eyebrows in confusion and tucked a stray bang behind her ear.

"Yeah, because for the next month or so you're going to be locked away in the studio recording your debut album."

"Oh," Elise laughed lightly though she was a little perturbed with how she could produce a whole album in just a month. She had six songs, seven at a push, which she'd written herself. But she'd need at least three more.

"You'll be working with some of the hottest producers," Jake continued, his eyes twinkling with excitement.

"Here at Cloud Records we want to give you the best possible sound we can. We're billing you as the next Claire Parry."

"Wow!" Elise breathed. Claire Parry was a huge pop star who wrote her own songs, went on world tours and always topped the Billboard charts. Elise, like most other young women, adored her stuff and idolized her. To even hear her name in the same breath as Claire Parry's was overwhelming.

"I know it might seem like everything is moving quickly," Jake sympathized. "But that's how it is in the music business. You don't stay hot for very long so we have to act quickly to get an album out there while you are still generating buzz."

"I'm generating buzz?" Elise still couldn't believe it all. She knew that her songs were going down well at the open mic nights but beyond that she doubted anyone had even heard of her. Her biggest fan was still her grandmother.

"You leave that to us," Jake grinned. He was a natural salesman. "We'll make you a star, you just focus on making great music."

"Okay," Elise nodded eagerly. "So when do we begin?"

***

Two weeks later and Elise stretched in the black leather chair and yawned.

"You can't be tired already," her producer, Antony, commented. He had black dreadlocks and a slight Jamaican accent.

Elise glanced at her watch.

"It's two in the morning," she groaned. "How can you not be tired?"

But she knew how Antony evaded the fatigue she was feeling. It was evident by the empty cans of Red Bull stacked up around him.

"We're in the race now," he chuckled to her. "We got to finish this 'ere album. I need you back in that booth laying vocals for 'Leave Me There.'"

Elise picked up her nearby bottle of water and drank thirstily from it. She'd never sung so much in all her life. Every day at eight a black city car picked her up and whisked her straight to the recording studio where she often stayed until three, sometimes four in the morning. She was operating on barely any sleep and was beginning to look and feel like a zombie.

Antony was kind, he let her nap on the sofas in the studio when he didn't need her input or her voice. But it was intense, much more intense than Elise could ever have anticipated. So much had changed in such a short space of time.

After her first day in the studio she was taken back to a part of the city she didn't recognize. Here, apparently, was her new apartment, purchased courtesy of the label. She finally had her own place, with private bedroom, stylish modern kitchen and vast open living area. It was fully furnished and beyond amazing. When Elise saw it she couldn't wait to have Dylan come around but she'd yet to find the time. When she wasn't locked up in the studio she was sleeping. But Dylan thankfully understood as his band was currently going through the exact same thing, locked up in a different studio on a different side of the city.

"Can I just have five minutes?" Elise asked Antony, yawning.

"Five minutes," he held up five fingers to her. "That's it."

Elise moved over onto the sofa and lifted her cell phone from her pocket. She pressed the speed dial for 1, which was reserved for Dylan.

"Hey," he answered after the sixth ring. His voice sounded groggy as though he'd been sleeping.

"Sorry, did I wake you?"

"Huh," she heard him knock something over. "Dammit. Urgh, yeah."

"Sorry," Elise repeated, feeling dreadful. They both had precious little time to sleep so she hated to disturb any rest he was able to have.

"Yeah, we got back at midnight as we killed it on a couple of tracks," Dylan explained, sounding a bit more awake.

"At midnight?" Elise felt her heart sink in her chest. That was over two hours ago. Why hadn't he called her when he got in? They were supposed to speak to one another every night before they fell asleep, no matter how late it was.

"I know I should have called," Dylan instantly apologized. "I meant to, I had my phone out and everything but I must have just crashed the moment I got in bed."

Elise understood how it could have happened. Lately she feared she might fall asleep while recording a song. The moment she was left alone she'd close her eyes and instantly be in a deep sleep.

"This is all so intense," she sighed. "I'm still at the studio."

"Still?"

"Yeah, I'm struggling on this one song, 'Leave Me There.' The vocals need to be quite raw and heartfelt and well…I'm just too exhausted to deliver."

On the other end of the line she could hear Dylan's deep, slow breathing.

"Dylan?"

"What?" he jolted back awake. "Shit, sorry, baby. I'm just so tired."

"It's okay, get some rest."

"Go kill that track," he told her. "I know you can do it."

"I love you," Elise whispered to him, holding the phone tenderly to her ear, savoring the sound of his voice.

"I love you too."

***

Elise wasn't sure if it was speaking to Dylan or just her own determination to get into bed and rest, but when she went back into the recording booth she sang 'Leave Me There' better than she ever had before. She fueled each line with all her emotion so that at the end she physically wilted against the microphone, completely drained.

"That was it!" Antony gushed, speaking to her from the other side of the glass. "You nailed it! We've got a hit record right there!"

"Great," Elise sighed. "Can I go home and sleep now?"

"I should think so."

***

Elise was being rewarded with a rare day off which meant she could sleep late into the day. She awoke at one in the afternoon to the sound of her front door buzzer screeching across the tranquility of her apartment. Groaning, she pulled herself out of bed, wrapped her pink terry cloth robe around her and hurried over in bare feet to the front door. She had a video phone so she could see whoever was calling her. She looked at the screen but the caller's face was obscured by an ornate bouquet of flowers.

"Who is it?" Elise pressed a button and spoke.

"Delivery," the caller replied gruffly. Elise rolled her eyes and pressed the button which opened her door.

"Okay, come on up."

Moments later there was a brisk knock at her front door. Elise opened it and saw the same bouquet of flowers, only more vibrant now than they had been on the screen. But as beautiful as the flowers were, it was the person behind them she was interested in. She spotted the leather sleeve and instantly knew it was him. She pushed the flowers aside and grinned in delight at Dylan.

"Hey, beautiful," he purred sexily at her. "I thought I'd come and surprise you, and reward you for making a hit last night."

He handed her the flowers and entered the apartment.

"So this is your new place?" He looked around approvingly. "It's awesome."

"Yeah," Elise shrugged modestly. "It's just nice to have my own bedroom now."

"Own bedroom?" Dylan arched an eyebrow in interest and Elise blushed.

"I should put these in water." She hurried over to the kitchen and turned on the cold water faucet.

"I didn't know you were off today," she called back to him as she placed the flowers in the sink to keep them fresh. She didn't yet have a vase within her apartment.

"I'm not," Dylan shrugged. "I managed to procure a prolonged lunch break."

"So you've got to go back after?" Elise couldn't conceal her disappointment. She'd been hoping they could spend the day together relaxing in her apartment, curling up on her sofa watching movies and eating takeout.

"Yep, 'fraid so," Dylan eyed her sadly. "We've still got three tracks to lay down by the end of the week."

"Well, I appreciate you coming to see me," Elise went to him and wrapped her arms around his neck. "Even if just for a little while." She leaned up towards him and softly kissed him on the lips.

"I've missed you," Dylan told her sincerely, stroking her cheek.

"I've missed you too," Elise rested her head against his chest. "Have you at least got time for me to go shower? I feel like a tramp because I just got up."

"Sure." Dylan removed his jacket and headed over to the sofa, across from which was hung an impressively large TV.

***

Elise hurriedly brushed her teeth and then stepped into her state-of-the-art waterfall shower. It took her a moment to get it working but finally it was cascading hot water down onto the stylish dark tiles. Elise removed her terry cloth robe and turquoise pajamas and stepped inside. The water upon her skin instantly felt cleansing. She pivoted happily beneath the stream, humming quietly to herself. Over the sound of the water she didn't hear the bathroom door open.

She jumped as two strong hands gripped her waist and spun her around. Dylan was in the shower. He was completely naked. He leaned down to kiss her. Elise was still in shock at his sudden presence but she couldn't deny him a kiss. As their lips connected his hands felt their way down her wet, bare body. Elise felt a thrill of delight dance down her spine and make her toes tingle. Their kiss deepened as the shower continued to soak them both.

"Do you want this?" Dylan asked breathily as he pulled away from her and whispered into her ear.

"Yes," Elise gasped. She knew that she wanted him more than anything. He was all she thought about.

Their bodies united beneath the torrent of hot water. Dylan was a skilled and sensitive lover. He pressed Elise up against the damp tiles and tenderly made love to her. Elise closed her eyes in euphoria. The sides of the shower steamed up, sealing them within their own cloud of hot, passionate love.

***

"So are you glad I stopped by?" Dylan grinned playfully as he wrapped a white towel around his toned torso. Elise couldn't stop gazing at his perfect chest.

"Hey, I'm not a piece of meat, you know," he quipped.

"I know," Elise blushed. "That was just all so…unexpected."

"In a good way?"

"In the best way," Elise reassured him, kissing him softly on the lips. They were both still flushed, and not just from the shower.

"I wish you could stay longer," Elise sighed. She wanted to never leave his arms.

"I know," Dylan gave her a sad smile. "But destiny awaits. We just need to complete these last few tracks, then things should calm down."

"Same for me."

"So we just finish our albums and then we'll have all the time in the world for each other," Dylan held her in his arms as he spoke.

"That sounds good," Elise agreed wistfully. Each minute she spent with Dylan was precious and every time they parted she yearned to be with him once again.

Chapter 8

"So we're really pleased with the album," Jake beamed to Elise as she sat across from him in the plush offices of Cloud Records.

"Oh, good," Elise sighed with relief. One month had extended to two but finally the album was recorded and being prepared for release. She was excited to have recorded her first album but more excited to now be able to spend more time with Dylan. She'd barely seen him while they had both been locked in the studio. But now both their albums were complete they'd have more time for one another.

"But now is when the real work starts," Jake warned her.

"The real work?" Elise repeated his words with unease. She'd been working every hour God sent for eight weeks straight. She was sleep deprived, exhausted and emotionally drained. She couldn't work any harder than she had, she had nothing left to give.

"Yes, now we need to start getting the word out about your album," Jake explained. Elise wasn't sure how this work would involve her; the label had always assured her that they'd handle the lion's share of the promotional work.

"Okay," she nodded at him, wondering what would be required of her next.

"We've actually been able to secure you a really exciting opportunity which should ensure your album's success."

"Oh?" Elise leaned forward expectantly in her chair. Was one of her songs going to be featured in a movie? Or in a TV commercial? She knew that many artists got their big break that way. It was a great way of getting your music heard by a broad audience.

"You're going to freak when we tell you!" Jake grinned.

"Okay, then tell me," Elise prompted.

"Guess who is going to be supporting Claire Parry on the European leg of her world tour?"

Elise had no idea. She shook her head.

"You!" Jake declared as he pointed a finger squarely at Elise.

"Me?" Elise couldn't believe it. Claire Parry was a huge star. And Europe! Elise had never even left America. Coming to New York was the first time she'd left her home state. She wasn't sure she was ready to visit an entirely new continent!

"Yes, you!" Jake clarified. "I told you it was a great opportunity! A chance to play your music live to thousands of fans every night! You must be thrilled."

"I am!" Elise nodded enthusiastically. And she was. But something soured what should have been a joyous moment. Dylan. It meant leaving Dylan. She wasn't sure if she could do that.

"How long would the tour be for?" she asked tentatively.

"Two months," Jake replied factually.

"Two months?" Elise's eyes widened. That would mean another two months away from Dylan, only this time she'd be in a different country, in a different time zone. He wouldn't be able to pop over with flowers when he had spare time. They'd be completely apart.

"Yep, and you leave tomorrow."

"Tomorrow?" Elise's head was spinning.

"Don't worry, we've got all your flights and hotels covered. You just need to pack and rest up."

Elise knew that she needed more than one night's sleep to rest up. Her body ached and she was beginning to forget small details like her phone number. She needed a good two weeks' rest to be back on top form. Each morning when she woke up it was becoming an increasing effort to drag herself out of bed.

"So go home, rest, get ready. Tomorrow is the first day of your big adventure."

***

"Two months?" Dylan cried in dismay as Elise delivered the news.

"I know," she sighed as she reached out and cupped his hands in hers. "But I couldn't pass it up, it's Claire Parry."

"Yeah, yeah, it's a great opportunity," Dylan agreed but she saw the disappointment etched on his handsome face. He squeezed her hands and gazed despondently at the television mounted on the wall which was currently playing the rental movie he'd brought for them to watch together.

Elise had tried to delay telling him and just focus on enjoying their date night. They'd ordered in pizza and planned on a romantic evening together, but then Dylan noticed her packed luggage by the front door and started asking questions. Elise knew that she owed him the truth.

"I just…I feel like I barely see you," he admitted sadly.

"I know," Elise pinched back tears. Every fiber in her being wanted to stay with him in New York. Instead she was jetting off the London, Paris, Milan. Places which had previously just been dots on a map to her.

"Two months without even seeing you," Dylan looked intently at her. His eyes bore into hers as though he could see right down into the depths of her soul.

"How will I cope?" he asked, forcing a slight smile.

"How will I cope?" Elise deflected as a solitary tear danced down her cheek. "I can't bear being apart from you."

Dylan reached out and embraced her, pulling her tightly into him. She breathed deeply, savoring his heady, cologne-laced scent. She wished she could bottle it up and take it with her and smell him each and every night she was away.

"We just met each other right at the start of our careers so it's tough," Dylan whispered to her.

"But it shouldn't be," Elise pulled back from him and wiped at her eyes. "It should be awesome and excited but I'm not enjoying any of it."

"What do you want me to do?" Dylan's look darkened. "Do you want me to set you free? To tell you to go follow your dreams and forget about me?"

"No!" Elise insisted, cupping his face in her hands.

"You are my dream," she told him sincerely. "You are more important to me than any of this."

"But I'd never ask you to give it up," Dylan gently lowered her hands from his face. "I don't want you to go back to being a waitress. I want you to be a superstar."

Elise sniffed tearfully.

"I'll be right here waiting for you when you get back off your tour," he promised her, sealing the promise with a soft kiss upon her lips.

"Can't you come with me?" she asked hopefully.

"I can't," Dylan sighed. "I still need to finish the band's album. We're already worryingly behind. I can just never motivate them. If they worked half as hard as you do we'd be done by now."

Elise heard the resentment in his voice. Things with his band were not going well.

"They just want the glamour and the fame," he continued. "They're not about the music, they're not willing to put in the work."

"Not everyone is as committed to being a rock star as you are," Elise smiled at him.

Dylan grinned at this but then abruptly stood up. He went over to her pile of luggage, including her guitar case, which he popped open. He removed her beloved guitar and came back over to the sofa. He sat down and positioned the guitar on his lap, his hands either side of it, ready to play.

He strummed a couple of notes, getting a feel for the instrument. Elise leaned against him, noticing how impossibly sexy he looked holding her guitar.

"I wish you didn't have to go," he sung gently to her. "But sometimes parting is good for the soul."

He continued to strum a sweet melody, inviting Elise to sing a few lines.

"I'll take you with me every step I take. Because this love is something distance can't break."

Together they jammed, singing a sweet song about parting but not saying goodbye. Outside the night darkened and the city became illuminated with a thousand streetlights glittering magically.

***

Elise awoke in bed to the sharp beeping of her alarm clock. Beside her Dylan was still sleeping. She could hear the steady rise and fall of his breath. Groaning, she propped herself up and leaned over to silence her alarm. It was still dark. She rubbed her eyes and wished that she could go back to sleep.

Quietly she crept from her bed and went to shower. When she emerged Dylan was undisturbed but she was running out of time. A car would soon arrive to take her to the airport. She left the bedroom and went out to her modern kitchen where she poured herself some cereal and made herself a fresh mug of coffee.

She sat eating from the bowl, with the city still twinkling beyond her window as the door to her bedroom creaked open and Dylan stumbled out, his dark hair matted around his head. He dropped down beside Elise and placed a hand upon her knee.

"You didn't say you had to get up so early," he told her, his voice groggy.

"I didn't want it to encroach on our time together." It had been after midnight when they'd eventually headed to bed. They watched the end of the movie, played the guitar and then made sweet music of a much more physical variety together.

"So you're going soon?" Dylan asked sadly.

"Yeah," Elise sighed and checked her watch. "I'm getting picked up at seven."

"When is your flight?"

"Nine."

Dylan groaned and buried his head in his hands.

"I don't want you to go," he admitted. "But I refuse to be the dick that asks you to say."

Elise understood how he felt. She wanted to stay, but she knew she couldn't. If she sacrificed her dream to be with a guy she wasn't sure she'd ever be able to forgive herself; her grandmother certainly wouldn't. Yet it felt wrong to be leaving Dylan. Their relationship was still so new, perhaps if they were more established it would be easier to leave.

Putting down her now empty bowl Elise picked up her guitar which was resting by the sofa. She ran her fingers along the strings, checking it was still in tune. Then she began to strum a popular melody which Dylan instantly recognized. He lifted his head to turn to her and smile.

"That's appropriate," he grinned.

"My mother used to sing this to me before bed," Elise explained. "It was her favorite song."

Then she kept playing and began to gently sing the song:

"Oh my bags are packed, I'm ready to go…"

Dylan leaned back and listened contentedly to her rendition of "Leaving on a Jet Plane." She sung with delicate, heartfelt emotion. It was beautiful to listen to.

"You know, I think I'll try to incorporate that into my set," Elise declared when she finished the song, her hand still resting by the strings, her fingertips itching to play some more.

"Really?"

"Yeah," Elise nodded. "And each time I play it, I'll dedicate it to you."

A Dream for Two

"You'd do that for me?" Dylan seemed incredibly touched by the gesture.

"Of course," Elise leaned forward and gently kissed him on the lips. "I love you, Dylan Cornish, and I want the whole world to know."

"I love you too," Dylan whispered as they kissed again. "What time are you getting picked up again?"

"Seven."

"So that gives us?" Dylan glanced down at her watch.

"Twenty minutes," Elise told him breathily.

"That's long enough!" Dylan playfully scooped her up into his arms and began carrying her back towards the bedroom. Elise squealed girlishly as he paused to spin her around. They were both laughing as he dropped her down into the center of the king-sized bed. Elise watched Dylan as he lowered himself towards her. Each time she saw him she felt like her heart might burst. By some miracle she'd found not only success in New York City but also true love. She just hoped that she'd still have both of those things when she returned from her eight-week tour. Dylan pressed his mouth against hers and as they kissed she momentarily forgot all about her problems and drifted away on the euphoria of his touch.

Chapter 9

Elise was still buzzing as she came off stage. The thunderous applause of the audience was ringing in her ears as she returned to her dressing room.

"You totally killed it," one of the stagehands excitedly told her.

"Thank you." Elise smiled modestly at them. As she wandered backstage towards her private dressing room she passed Claire Parry. She was wearing an ornate dress adorned with thousands of sequins and had silver fairy wings strapped to her back. She'd make her entrance by descending onto the stage as though she were flying down to it. The audience adored seeing it and Elise would always hear their cheerful cries as she sat and began removing her stage makeup.

"Another great set," Claire complimented her, smiling out from her own heavily made-up face covered in glitter and silver lipstick.

"Thank you." Elise blushed. Each time she saw Claire she had to pinch herself that this was all real and actually happening.

"Are you coming out with us all for drinks after the show?" Claire asked, as she did each time they passed in the corridors.

"Not tonight."

"You going to be phoning that boy of yours?" Claire grinned as Elise nodded numbly. "He must be some guy to be able to compete with all of this!" Claire exclaimed. "He must be a keeper."

"Yeah," Elise nodded. "He is."

In the relative quiet of her dressing room Elise unzipped her skinny jeans, chucked off her glittery t-shirt and pulled on a waiting flannel jumpsuit which felt comfortable and homey. Then she started to remove all the makeup which had been plastered onto her face. She was always given heavy, smoky eyes and nude lips. This would apparently be her look. Her appearance was much more stripped down than Claire Parry's, which made it easier for the audience to differentiate between them and their sounds. Claire played high-energy pop songs but Elise's were now stripped back and more rustic in sound.

Once the makeup was off Elise would call Dylan. Since she was now in Europe timing was an issue. Depending on where she was she could be six or seven hours ahead of Dylan. She was currently in France which put her six hours ahead. So while it was almost nine in the evening for her, for Dylan it was just three in the afternoon. He should be at the studio recording. Elise dialed his number and waited expectantly for him to answer.

He picked up after the third ring. "Hey, beautiful! How did your show go?"

"Amazing," Elise gushed. "I'm still shaking."

"I bet it never gets old," Dylan said softly.

"I wish you were here to see it though."

"Yeah, me too."

For a moment the line went quiet as they were each briefly lost to contemplation. It had been three weeks since they'd seen one another.

"Hey, I saw you on TV today!" Dylan suddenly declared brightly.

"On TV?"

"Yeah, your new music video aired. It's awesome, Elise. Everyone already loves it!"

"Oh, that's great." Elise felt a little deflated. She'd wanted to witness her music video airing for the first time, not be on another continent when it happened. She knew she could go online and track people's reactions to the video but it wasn't the same as experiencing it firsthand. It was like watching someone else's life unfold. Being on tour left her feeling detached from what was going on back home.

A Dream for Two

"It's a great video," Dylan insisted.

"I'll have to watch it."

Then they talked about their day. Dylan would vent about how his band's album was still incomplete. They had one last track to lay down but the band members were struggling to agree on a concept for the song. When Elise listened, it made her feel grateful that she was a solo artist and didn't have to clear her music with anyone else.

As they talked she'd close her eyes and pretend that Dylan was right there beside her. She'd picture him, casually strewn across a nearby chair, wearing his leather jacket, his head tilted to the side. But when she opened her eyes and found the chair empty she always felt a plunging feeling of sadness taint her entire evening. Despite all her success, really all she wanted was to be sharing it with Dylan.

Elise often yawned as the conversation came to an end. Life on the road was exhausting and she slept every chance she could. So often they were traveling through the night on the bus, desperately trying to reach the next concert venue on time.

"You should get some rest," Dylan heard the yawn.

"I'm okay," Elise replied as she rubbed sleepily at her eyes. She heard a loud cheer shake the walls of her dressing room. Claire had clearly just landed on the stage in her fairy attire.

"We'll talk more tomorrow," Dylan promised her. "I love you."

"I love you, too."

Only they never did get to talk more the following day. As the tour progressed they ended up talking less and less. As Elise kept more obscure hours, when she did manage to call Dylan he rarely answered. And each time he called her back she was sleeping and missed her calls. They were what her grandmother would refer to as ships passing in the night. And Elise knew that wasn't a good thing. She wondered if her grandmother could hear her pain in her voice when they spoke.

"How's it all going over there?" her grandmother would ask, raising her voice even though she didn't have to, as though she didn't trust the phone networks to successfully carry her message across an entire ocean.

"Fine, Grandma. I'm enjoying it."

"You sound tired," her grandmother accurately noted. "Are you tired?"

"A bit, I guess." Elise was exhausted.

"Are you eating enough?"

"I'm eating fine."

"I know some of that foreign food can be strange. When you get back here I'll feed you up with my meatloaf and cornbread."

"Sounds good, Grandma."

"I went to the library and watched your music video on that YouTube thing."

"You did?" This surprised Elise. Her grandmother usually seemed allergic to all technology.

"I did," her grandmother stated proudly. "Had one of the girls there get me all set up. I watched your video and read all the lovely things people have said about it. You've got a gift, Elise, and you're sharing it with the world. Your ma would be so proud."

Elise blinked back tears. She didn't want to think about her parents. They were just someone else who should be witnessing all that was happening to her but couldn't be there. She wasn't sure her heart had the capacity to miss anyone else. Missing Dylan alone felt all consuming at times.

"Don't be sad," her grandmother urged her. "Be happy. You're doing something wonderful, Elise. Enjoy it."

"I am," Elise wiped at her tired eyes.

"And you'll be home soon."

"Yeah," Elise sighed contentedly. "I'll be home soon."

***

It had been almost two weeks since Elise had spoken to Dylan. They'd exchanged messages but that wasn't the same. She wanted to hear his voice. Wanted to close her eyes and imagine him close. But as her plane touched down at JFK airport she was at least back in the same country, same state even, as he was. Soon they'd be reunited. The moment she left the plane Elise powered up her phone and told him she was headed back to her apartment and that she couldn't wait to see him. She hoped he felt the same. Two weeks was a long time to go without speaking.

Elise dragged her bags out to a waiting town car. Some people within the airport recognized her and cautiously approached her for an autograph. Elise was still suffering from jet lag and so in a daze she posed for pictures and thanked them for their kind words about her music. It was bizarre that she'd left New York an unknown and was arriving back a star. Since she'd been away her first music video had debuted and her album was up for preorder. Everything was happening.

But all Elise cared about was seeing Dylan again. She leaned back in the quiet of the car and counted the number of streets she'd need to pass before she reached her apartment where he'd supposedly be waiting for her.

Finally Elise hauled her bags into the elevator of her apartment building and climbed out at her floor. As she headed down the corridor she felt her heart sink. There was no sign of Dylan. She'd expected him to be waiting at her door with a huge smile for her. Instead her doorway was empty. Forlornly she unlocked it and walked inside. As she did so she looked around and dropped her luggage in surprise. It released a heavy thud as it landed by her feet but she didn't care. She was staring around wide-eyed at her apartment which had been transformed.

There were candles everywhere. They were strewn across the floor and on every available surface. They flickered magically in the darkness of the apartment as the drapes had been sealed and the lights shut off. And also scattered everywhere were rose petals. It was overwhelmingly beautiful, like a scene out of a movie. But the best part was standing in the center of it all.

"Dylan!" Elise cried with joy as she ran into his outstretched arms. They kissed and she melted against him.

"I've missed you so much," she cried as they eventually parted.

"I've missed you too," Dylan told her fondly as he tenderly stroked her cheek. "I hope you don't mind but I wanted to surprise you. The building's super let me in."

"I don't mind at all," Elise gushed. "It's...beautiful."

And it was. The candlelight made everything seem magical and wondrous. She kissed Dylan again, harder this time. It was a kiss filled with longing and desire. Despite her jet lag and exhaustion she wanted him. Her body burned with yearning to be in his arms, to feel his naked skin against hers.

***

Lifting her head Elise saw that some of the surrounding candles had nearly burned out. After making love she'd rested her head upon Dylan's bare chest and fallen asleep. Even though they were on the floor she didn't care. She'd be comfortable anywhere with him.

"This is just like a fairy tale," she whispered to him.

"That would make you Sleeping Beauty," Dylan smiled at her in the candlelight. "You drooled all over my chest."

"I did?!" Elise blushed.

"It's okay," Dylan sat up and gently tucked some loose hair behind her ears. "I don't mind. I'm just glad you got to rest a bit."

"I'm just so happy to be back," Elise wrapped her arms around his neck and kissed him lightly on the lips.

"Now that I'm back we can finally enjoy New York together. We can actually spend some proper time together!"

"About that," Dylan grabbed her hands and lifted them off him. He looked sad. Elise felt panic pinch at her heart. What was wrong? Was he breaking up with her? Had she been gone too long, did he feel too abandoned by her?

"I'd love to stay here in New York with you," he told her sincerely. "But I can't. I wanted to tell you sooner but I didn't want to ruin your homecoming."

"Tell me what?" Elise demanded, struggling to remain calm.

"I have to leave tomorrow," Dylan sighed despairingly. "The band is going on tour with Tom Sheehan. We're supporting his U.S. tour. We'll be going all over the country for the next six weeks."

Elise was speechless. She knew she couldn't go with him, not that he'd even asked her. Her next weeks were full of promotional commitments, TV and radio appearances and interviews.

"I don't want you to go," she whispered as tears streaked down her cheeks. But she knew she couldn't ask him to stay, as much as she wanted to. Because she'd already left him to follow her dream, she couldn't deny him that same opportunity.

Chapter 10

Without Dylan, New York had lost its sparkle. It had been ten days since his band had left to go on tour. Elise was struggling without him. Everything in the city reminded her of him; from the scent of the hot dog vendors on the street to the steam rising up from the sewer vents. They were all things which she'd originally experienced with Dylan. She kept thinking what he'd say if he were there with her, how he'd react to things.

When she was on tour it was easier to get by. She was in a new place, exhausted from all the traveling. Time seemed to move quicker, meaning she didn't get the chance to miss him as much as she now was. Even her apartment was just bursting with reminders of him. Each time Elise walked through the door she remembered how it felt to see the candles and flowers he'd lovingly arranged for her. Knowing that her apartment was now just empty and there was no one there to greet her was becoming unbearable.

"He'll be back before you know it," Gloria reassured her over hot chocolate at a boutique café, Elise's treat.

Gloria had been so kind and understanding of her friend's newfound success while she still was attending numerous auditions in her free time and had no luck.

"I know," Elise smiled thinly.

"And I bet he's missing you as much as you miss him."

"I doubt it," Elise sighed. "I bet he's so busy with the tour that he barely gets a chance to think about me at all."

"Don't be silly!" Gloria chastised her. "I bet he thinks about you all the time. He probably wrote a new song all about you!"

"I just keep worrying that he's going to meet someone and do something stupid," Elise admitted forlornly. Spending so much time alone with her thoughts meant that negative ones were beginning to grow and nest, polluting all the positive ones like a virus.

"He loves you, Elise. He won't do anything to jeopardize that."

"But girls throw themselves at him," Elise gazed sadly at her hot, sweet drink.

"So?" Gloria questioned. "It doesn't mean he can't throw the skanks back off!"

This made Elise laugh.

"See, you can still smile!" Gloria pointed a perfectly manicured fingernail at her.

"Yeah, seems I can."

"You got to keep smiling. Things are always darkest before the dawn, you got to remember that. It's what I'm always telling myself."

Gloria was still working shifts at the diner. She hadn't been able to hand in her notice as Elise had.

"How are your auditions going?" Elise asked tentatively. She knew how long and how hard Gloria had been chasing her dream of becoming an actress.

"Nothing," Gloria shook her head and for a moment her cheerful demeanor gave way to how she truly felt. But ever the actress, she quickly pasted a smile back on her face and grinned across the table at her friend.

"But, hey, things can only get better, right?" she asked brightly.

"Yeah."

"Besides, I'm actually thinking about moving to L.A."

"L.A.? Are you serious?" Elise suddenly felt panicked. She couldn't be left in the city without both her boyfriend and her best friend. She'd be completely alone.

"Yeah," Gloria nodded. "It's been on my mind for some time. There's more opportunities out there, more TV work and stuff."

Elise wasn't within that industry but what Gloria said made sense. Most films and television shows were produced in California, so a majority of the acting work to be had was out there.

"But I don't want you to leave," Elise told her sincerely.

"I know," Gloria smiled fondly at her. "You didn't want Dylan to leave, either. But you've got to let people chase their dreams."

"I know," Elise took a sip of her hot chocolate. "And you'll become the star you're supposed to be in L.A.!"

"Exactly," Gloria laughed. "I'll be polishing my Oscar in no time at all!"

Elise was about to say something when someone tapped her on the shoulder. She turned and was faced with a giggling collection of tweens who were staring at her, cell phones poised, their eyes wide with nervous expectation.

"Hi, are you Elise Roberts?" the tallest of them asked.

"Um, yeah, that's me," Elise confirmed.

"Oh, my God, I told you!" the girl gushed as her friends around her screamed in delight. Elise felt her cheeks burn as people began to look over and stare at the commotion.

"We like, love your music," the tall girl told her enthusiastically. "Can we please take a picture with you?"

"Yeah, of course." Elise smiled politely as the girls gathered around her and released an abundance of flashes in her face as they captured their desired images.

"I can't believe it's really you!" another girl gushed.

"Aren't you dating Dylan Cornish?" the tall girl asked. "He's like so hot," she added before Elise had chance to respond. The girls began chattering among themselves about Dylan and his band. They waved zealously at Elise as they walked away, poring over their cell phones and their new pictures.

"Well, that was weird," Elise tucked her hair shyly behind her ear and glanced back at her friend.

"But that's what I want," Gloria sighed wistfully. "I want to be bothered by overexcited tweens when I'm out having a hot chocolate."

Elise wanted to tell her that it wasn't as ideal as she thought it was but she held her tongue. She was living her dream, she didn't want to ever forget that and take it for granted. Gloria was still chasing hers but she'd get there, Elise knew she was talented enough to become a huge movie star.

"So, L.A. here I come," Gloria raised her mug in a toast.

"L.A. had better be ready for its next big star," Elise smiled at her as she knocked her mug against hers.

***

The tour bus stank. Dylan rolled over in his tiny bunk bed and tried not to inhale the accumulated scent of four grown men living in close proximity to one another. He wasn't sure what time it was. Time lost all meaning on the bus. They just rolled from state to state, gig to gig. He slept in a tiny bunk which could barely contain his six-foot physique and showered in the cramped bathroom inside the bus. Sometimes as a treat their tour manager booked them a hotel suite when they stayed in one place long enough so that they could stretch their legs and enjoy a proper shower.

He'd been living on the tour bus for over a week. Already Dylan was tired of the monotony. After each gig the band piled on to the bus and began drinking. His band mates would drink until they reached oblivion and collapsed in various places around the bus. But Dylan didn't want to just drink, he wanted to call Elise, to hear how she was doing but he had no privacy. Each time he called her they'd gather around him, teasing him and shouting out obscenities. They were all single. Their single status was the root cause of another issue on the bus: groupies.

Each night a new stream of overeager female fans followed them onto the bus to partake in drinking games. Often they ended up engaging in a sexual act with one or more band members. They'd even throw themselves at Dylan, telling him that it was okay, that no one would know. But he'd know and he loved Elise. She deserved his loyalty.

His bunk was pretty much the only place he could escape the rest of the band. He hated being in there, it was so cramped and he could barely move but it was his space and he could sort of be alone. Lying there he'd text Elise and tell her how he was getting on, which state he was in. He was trying to buy her a little souvenir of each place he visited. He wanted to present them all to her when he was back in New York as sort of a visual guide to his tour. He missed her so much it made his whole body ache. Each time something funny happened he wanted to share it with her, to see her face light up. Instead he was surrounded by his horny band mates who only wanted to drink and get laid.

Lying back, Dylan held his cell phone a few inches above his head and texted Elise. He told her how much he missed her, how much he loved her as the bus rolled towards Denver, the next stop of their tour.

***

"This is your schedule for today," Jake handed Elise a piece of paper with a neatly typed list. Her day would be consisting of almost two dozen radio interviews, all conducted from the Cloud Records studio. It was going to be a long day. Elise scanned the list and nodded at him.

"Okay, that looks fine."

"There's just one thing we need to discuss," Jake leaned towards her and clasped his hands together. Elise saw the look in his eyes and knew that whatever he had to say, it wouldn't be good. But she hadn't done anything wrong, had she? She thought she'd done everything the label had asked of her.

"Oh?" Elise braced herself.

"When in interview you're asked whether you're dating anyone, just say you're single." Jake's voice was low and non-confrontational. Nevertheless Elise could feel herself flying into a rage.

"But I'm not single!" she insisted. "I'm dating Dylan Cornish."

"I know," Jake appeared pained by her response. "But you see, it's not good for your image to be dating, especially not the front man of a punk rock group. Dylan's band has a reputation and not a good one. We are promoting you as this pure Southern belle, a sultry songbird if you will. It won't work if you are dating someone like Dylan Cornish."

"So you're asking me to lie?" Elise asked as she blinked back tears. It felt so wrong. In interviews people were specifically trying to find out more about her. What sort of a person would she be if she gave them false information which was then fed back to her fans? She'd be a fraud!

"Just bend the truth," Jake put on his salesman smile as he addressed her. "It's all about your image, Elise, your brand."

Elise could feel her cheeks burning. How would Dylan feel if he tuned in to listen to an interview with her and she was denying they were even together? She'd be distraught if he did that to her.

"You need to distance yourself from Dylan Cornish," Jake declared warningly, his friendly demeanor suddenly gone.

"He's bad for your image, Elise, and will be bad for your career. I suggest you end whatever you have with him and soon. You need to focus on your music now, nothing else."

Elise absorbed the words numbly and followed Jake towards the studio where she'd be sitting and answering interview questions for hours.

Chapter 11

Dylan placed his earbuds in his ears and wriggled down in his bunk bed, a content smile settling upon his handsome face. He'd seen on Elise's Twitter page that she was scheduled to give an interview with the radio station he was currently listening to and he couldn't wait to hear her soft voice speaking out across the miles to him.

The tour bus was currently driving down a highway, en route to the next stop on the tour. All his band mates were sleeping, curled up beside their latest conquests so at least Dylan wouldn't be mocked for listening to the interview.

"Here at Digital D-40 Radio Station we are crazy excited to have new singing sensation Elise Roberts here with us for an interview! Good afternoon, Elise," the bubbly presenter opened the interview.

"Good afternoon," Elise replied in her soft Southern drawl. Dylan grinned when he heard her and rolled onto his side, wishing he could focus on her voice and pretend she was there beside him.

"You're on a roller-coaster ride to stardom which just seems to go up and up!" the broadcaster commented excitedly.

"Yes, I've been really lucky," Elise said modestly. She sounded so sweet. Dylan could feel himself swelling with pride.

"You've got a host of new fans, an amazing new song and a fantastic debut album about to be released. But first, for everyone out there dying to know, put us out of our misery; Elise, are you seeing anyone special?"

There was a brief moment of silence. Then Elise replied in her sugary Southern voice:

"No, I'm single."

Dylan froze. He listened to the rest of the interview but he didn't hear anything she said. All he could think about was how she'd publicly denied him like that. Did she truly believe that she was single? As hot tears pricked at his blue eyes, making them glisten, he pulled his earphones from his ears and rolled out of his bunk.

He was thankful that everyone else was resting. He didn't want them quizzing him about what was wrong. He stormed over to the fridge and pulled out a cool bottle of beer. He popped the top and began to greedily down the contents. As he drank the curtain of one of the bunks opened and a pair of long, lean legs came out.

A Dream for Two

A platinum blonde wearing hot pants and a bra sauntered over to Dylan. She sat down on the nearby sofa and batted her false eyelashes at him.

"Hey," she purred the greeting at him.

"Hey," Dylan replied a little abruptly. He was in no mood to make small talk. He leaned down and grabbed a second bottle of beer from the fridge.

"Having a rough night?" the blonde asked with a knowing smile.

"Something like that," Dylan muttered. He dropped down next to her and drank from his bottle of beer.

She coyly crossed and then uncrossed her long legs, allowing Dylan to see just how toned and tanned they were. Then she leaned towards him and ran a hand down his back.

"You look like you shouldn't be alone tonight," she whispered directly into his ear.

***

Elise nodded at the instruction her producer had given her even though she hadn't taken in what he'd said. They were working on a remix for her next track but she couldn't concentrate. Every other second she was checking her phone to see if Dylan had called. She'd heard nothing from him in over a week and she was starting to fear that something terrible had happened. Despite her numerous texts and calls she heard nothing in response. The more time that passed the worse Elise began to feel about everything.

"Again, please, from the top," the producer's voice bounced around the recording booth. He sounded annoyed.

"Okay," Elise nodded and willed herself to focus. The music started up again and she nodded along, counting herself in. But still she was thinking about Dylan. Why hadn't he called her? What if he'd heard one of those awful radio interviews she'd had to give and now hated her? What if he'd left her? She wasn't single. She kept telling him as much in her messages. She explained how Jake had told her to say that, how it was about protecting her image, but as she wrote the words she realized how low she had sunk. She was lying about being in love just to sell records. She hated herself. This wasn't the sort of person she'd wanted to become.

"Elise, focus, you missed your cue!" the producer shouted at her.

Wiping her eyes Elise nodded through him at the glass and apologized for the fourth time.

"Don't apologize, just sing the damn song like we rehearsed," he told her.

Elise didn't blame him for being angry. She was wasting everyone's time at the studio including her own simply because she couldn't stop thinking about Dylan. If only he'd call her and tell her what was going on with him. It was the not knowing which was killing her. But if he did decide to leave her she wouldn't blame him. She'd done a terrible thing.

"Shit, Elise, you missed it again!" The producer was clearly past the point of annoyed and had reached angry. Elise removed her headphones and walked out of the booth. She couldn't do it. It was taking all the strength she had to hold herself together.

"I'm sorry," she sniffed at her angry producer as she collected together her things and prepared to leave.

"I just can't do this today."

She heard him ranting at her as she left but she ignored him. She just had to get home and get away from the rest of the world so that she could safely think of only Dylan.

***

Back in her apartment Elise ran a bubble bath and climbed in. She hoped that the cherry-scented bubbles which now engulfed her would help wash away some of her troubles. What else could she do about Dylan? She'd left numerous voicemails and messages explaining herself, all of which had been ignored.

She placed her cell phone on the floor near the bathtub just in case Dylan called while she was bathing. Lately her phone was basically glued to her hip as she lived in fear of missing his call. She just wanted to speak to him, to get a chance to properly apologize. She knew she'd messed up. Her career wasn't worth losing him over, she should never have lied.

Lying back in the bubbles she began to relax a little. The warmth of the water massaged her aching limbs and helped relieve some of her tension. Her eyes had just flickered closed when she was jolted awake by the sharp trill of her cell phone. Desperately she splashed around in the water as she reached for the device and pressed it eagerly against her damp ear without even checking who the incoming call was from.

"Hello?" she asked, praying that it was Dylan on the other end of the line.

"Oh, so you're alive then?" Jake retorted coldly. Elise felt herself physically wilt upon hearing his voice. She instantly regretted having picked up.

"Look, about earlier–" she began to explain but Jake cut her off.

"No need to explain, Elise. I know what's happening, I've seen it a thousand times before. You're getting too big for your boots. You think that one hit record does a star make? Well trust me, honey, it doesn't. If you want to stay on top you've got to be prepared to work and to work hard. Do you think Claire Parry got to where she is by walking out of recording sessions?"

Elise wanted to object, to point out that she had never been one to shy away from hard work and she certainly hadn't gotten too big for her boots. But she knew how bad her walkout looked and so she kept quiet and allowed Jake to vent at her.

"We need you to be as committed as we are," he continued. "We can't put all this time, money and effort into you only to have you flake on us."

"It won't happen again," Elise promised him.

"Good," Jake sounded relieved. "I mean, what is it you need? A couple of days off? Some r and r? Take a long weekend, I can book you into one of New York's top spas. Then we hit the studio first thing Tuesday with you new and refreshed. What do you think?"

"Sounds good." Elise wasn't sure how her walking out warranted a long weekend and a spa break. She reasoned that Jake was just desperately trying to keep his starlet happy. She'd heard rumors of how difficult other recording artists could be to work with. The word temperamental was used a lot.

"Okay, great," Jake's voice slowed down as he was clearly satisfied with the conclusion to their conversation. What bemused Elise was that he never once stopped to ask her if something was actually wrong. For all he knew there might have been a death in the family. But all he cared about was getting her back in the studio and making him money as quickly as possible.

"Thanks for understanding," Elise hoped she had sounded sarcastic but was pretty sure she'd failed. She only ever sounded sweet. Jake hung up and she angrily tossed her phone across the floor. It skittered across the dark tiles and eventually stopped. Elise dropped back down into her sea of bubbles.

"Oh, Dylan," she forlornly called out his name. "Why haven't you called me?"

She wished she could ask Gloria for advice but her friend was already on the opposite side of the country, making a go of things in L.A. She'd sent Elise a few video messages, bragging about the abundance of sunshine and hot guys there. Elise smiled as she watched them, her friend genuinely seemed happy, the L.A. lifestyle seemed to suit her. And she apparently had a load of auditions lined up which was always a good thing.

Elise closed her eyes and tried to relax and stop stressing over what was, or wasn't, happening with Dylan.

***

Wrapped in her terry cloth robe Elise wandered forlornly around her main living area. With a glass of wine in hand she looked out at the city from her main window. A thousand lights sparkled in the early evening darkness. Each light represented another apartment, another person, another life. But despite being surrounded by all these people Elise felt completely alone.

Below her numerous cars snaked their way along the streets, many drivers resorting to angrily hammering on their horns. When she'd first arrived the level of noise had shocked her but now she was so used to it that she barely noticed it at all. The car horns, the shouting, the screech of sirens just felt like background noise now. If the world suddenly stilled and was silent, as it was back at her grandmother's of an evening, she wasn't sure how she'd feel, probably on edge. At her grandmother's all you heard at night was the gentle sound of crickets calling out for one another. It was such a peaceful place. Elise's life had been simpler back then. She'd been stuck in a job she loathed but she'd been happy. She hadn't known then how it felt to have your heart broken, how dangerous it was to love someone so completely that they became like oxygen and without them you couldn't breathe.

Leaning forward Elise breathed onto the glass of her window. Her breath misted and raising a finger, she drew a loose heart and within it the initials E and D and beneath that the word "4eva." Then she kissed the image. No matter what happened, she would always love Dylan Cornish. He was a part of her now. She just hoped that deep down, he knew that.

Chapter 12

Elise pressed her face tightly against her pillow and sealed her eyes shut. The knock came again at her apartment door, this time more persistent. Whoever it was she didn't want to see them, they could just go away. She figured it was probably Jake, coming round to see why she hadn't attended her spa day which he'd arranged for her. But she couldn't go. A few back rubs and scented candles wouldn't help her get over the fact that she'd seemingly lost Dylan.

Rolling on to her side Elise tightened herself into a ball and burrowed deeply beneath her duvet. She wished she could shut out the entire world and have nothing exist beyond the reassuring comfort of her bed. Her eyes ached from crying and she was sick of constantly checking her phone for messages and being continually disappointed. If Dylan hadn't got in touch by now then it was obvious that he wasn't going to.

When she wasn't sulking in bed she was stalking his band's movements on line. She saw through their Twitter account that they were now in California as part of their tour. Elise considered calling Gloria and asking her to check in on Dylan but she decided against it. A part of her was too terrified to discover if he'd gotten over her, if he'd already moved on to someone else.

According to their online presence the band members were having a great time. There were pictures of them partying hard on their tour bus. There was an image of Dylan holding a bottle of beer and grinning directly into the camera. He looked so happy and carefree, not like a guy who had just lost the love of his life. Elise knew what it all meant. She wished he would just call her and give her closure. She felt like she was living in some strange limbo where she couldn't let go of the faint hope that perhaps he did still love her, that perhaps they were actually still together. If she hoped hard enough, maybe it would come true?

Elise hugged her legs against her chest and sighed deeply.

The knocking came a third time.

"Go away!" Elise yelled dramatically although she doubted that they could hear her from her bed. If she wanted them to leave she'd have to answer the door. Groaning she threw off her duvet and stood up. She was wearing her favorite shorty pajamas. She hadn't taken them off for almost forty-eight hours. All of the curtains were drawn in her apartment, casting everywhere in unnatural darkness. She didn't want to see the sunlight. It wasn't welcome there.

Yawning, she moved through the shadows covering her apartment towards the front door. She was so indifferent to whoever was standing on the other side that she didn't even bother to check the digital caller screen. Instead she just unlocked the latch and threw open her door.

"Yes?" she asked tersely, anticipating that she'd find Jake there pretending to be concerned about her welfare.

But where Jake should have been standing was someone holding a huge bouquet of white lilies. The arrangement of flowers was so huge that it obscured the delivery guy's face. Elise eyed the flowers dubiously. Were they from the label to placate her for her recent seemingly ill-tempered behavior? She didn't need pity petals.

"I'm not expecting a delivery," Elise was about to shut the door when a familiar voice quipped:

"I thought girls always wanted flowers."

Elise felt her heart seize in her chest. Was it him?

The lilies were slightly lowered to reveal the man holding them. Elise gasped in delight when she saw Dylan's sparkling blue eyes and his thick dark hair.

"Dylan!" she uttered his name, growing tearful. But why was he there? His band was currently in California performing a number of sold-out gigs. The tour was a roaring success, surely they needed their front man?

Pushing all her questions out of her mind Elise stepped outside and allowed Dylan and the lilies into her apartment. She saw him glance around and take in the relative darkness.

"Did you turn into a vampire while I was away?" he asked, smirking slightly.

Elise laughed and then looked down at her pajamas which she'd been living in for two whole days. She suddenly felt unbearably gross. She sneakily cupped a hand over her mouth and checked her breath and hoped that her hair wasn't too crazy.

"Anyway, these are for you," Dylan shyly handed her the flowers. Elise took them from him and inhaled deeply. The collection of lilies smelled heavenly.

"They are beautiful," she gushed. "Thank you so much."

She carried them over to her kitchen area and then glanced back at Dylan.

"But I don't feel like I deserve flowers," she admitted, her shoulders slumping. "And how are you even here? Aren't you meant to be in California?"

Dylan's jaw clenched at the influx of questions.

"I'm sorry, I know I've no right to pry."

"No, you've every right to pry," Dylan came over and placed his strong hands upon her slender shoulders.

"You're my girlfriend," he declared proudly. "It's a girlfriend's prerogative to pry."

"So I'm still your girlfriend?" Elise melted beneath his touch as tears misted her eyes.

"Of course," he gave her a sexy, lopsided smile.

"But what about what I said on the radio?"

"It's okay," Dylan told her soothingly. "I understand why you did it."

Elise could no longer meet his gaze, she felt too ashamed.

"The label kept putting the same pressure on me," Dylan continued. "They said it would help the band's image if we were all single and seemingly playing the field."

Dylan drew Elise into him and she rested her head against his shoulder. She inhaled deeply, intoxicated by his scent which she'd missed so dearly. For a moment they just stood in one another's arms, relishing how it felt to be together again. But eventually Elise leaned back so that she could look up into his piercing blue eyes.

"But why are you here?" she wondered aloud. "I mean, shouldn't you be with the band?"

"Yeah, I should," Dylan nodded.

"Then why are you here?" Elise repeated. It made no sense. They had a gig that very evening, he'd never make it back to California on time to perform.

"I quit the band."

"What?" Elise pushed him away from her and stared at him in shock. "You quit the band?"

"Yeah," Dylan shrugged nonchalantly and shoved his hands into his jean pockets.

"Why?" Elise cried. "Why would you do that?"

"Because I realized the price I'd have to pay if I stayed in the band." He took a step towards Elise and cupped her face in his hands.

"If I stayed in the band I risked losing you."

"But the band was your dream!" Elise insisted.

"No," Dylan shook his head and smiled wistfully at her. "The band was my dream once. But it was never really about the band, it was about the music. And I can still love music whether or not I'm in the band. But I have a new dream now. And my new dream is you."

He leaned towards her and their lips met. Elise swore she felt a spark tingle her bottom lip as they came together and kissed. She'd missed the power of his kisses. Dylan cupped her face tightly as he kissed her.

The kiss reverberated throughout Elise's entire body, making her tingle all over. It was the sort of kiss which left you weak at the knees.

"Dylan," she breathed his name dreamily as they parted. She'd been so terrified that she'd lost him, that she'd made too grave a mistake to rectify in saying publicly that she was single.

"What will you do now?" she wondered.

"Let's leave tomorrow's problems for tomorrow," Dylan suggested. Taking her by the hand he led her through the apartment, towards her bedroom.

They stayed in there, locked in passionate embraces for two days. When Elise finally emerged bleary-eyed and euphoric, she threw open her curtains and finally let in the warming rays of sunlight. The sun streaked across her apartment, bathing everywhere in golden light. It gave the whole place an almost ethereal look.

In her bedroom she and Dylan had formulated a plan. A plan which would allow them both to pursue their dreams of a music career but also be together. And Elise realized now that being together was the main goal, as what good was a dream if you had no one to share it with? She felt full of purpose and her whole body glowed with joy. She hummed to herself as she turned on the kettle and prepared some blueberry pancakes for Dylan.

A Dream for Two

They had a plan and it was a great one. Now they just had to go out into the world and execute it.

Chapter 13

"No! Absolutely not!" Jake cried fervently from across the meeting table. "It would be total career suicide!"

"I don't agree," Elise shook her head stubbornly.

"Elise, sweetheart," he tried to reason with her. "You don't understand the industry like I do. You are all set to be a great solo artist, why rock the boat now?"

"Because I know it's the right thing to do," Elise said with certainty.

Jake bunched his hands into fists in frustration.

"A male and female duet hasn't hit the big time since Sonny and Cher!" he seethed.

"We'll make it," Elise smiled sweetly.

"Elise, please reconsider," Jake pleaded. "I'd hate to see all your talent go to waste."

"My talent isn't going to waste," Elise scowled at him. "I'm actually expanding on it."

"The cost to re-record your album with him on it will be extortionate," Jake let his head fall into his hands in despair.

"As we negotiated, any additional costs can be taken against future royalties," Elise replied factually.

"But there will be no future royalties!" Jake lamented. "That's what I'm trying to tell you!"

"I think you underestimate the music-buying public," Elise told him calmly. "People want to hear great music filled with passion, and that's what Dylan and I have."

"You have passion in the bedroom, maybe, but on a record? Do you know how difficult it is to capture that? It's like lightning in a bottle!"

"Well then, we're just going to have to try."

***

Being in the recording studio with Dylan was a completely different experience than recording alone. Elise no longer cared that she was inside all day, sitting in a booth. She laughed so hard her cheeks ached and sang with more depth and emotion than ever before. It was as if having Dylan there amplified everything that was good in her. She wanted their recording sessions to never end.

They re-recorded her whole album as duets and then added a new song, one they had penned together about making love survive. They called it "Endure." It was to be the first single they released as a couple.

"I can't believe we are actually doing this together," Dylan gushed excitedly as he wrapped an arm around Elise's waist and stood waiting to be called on set to record their music video. A warehouse outside New York had been transformed to look like a Parisian street and both Elise and Dylan were already in costume.

"I know," Elise declared dreamily as she leaned against him.

"I mean, does this even look like Paris?" Dylan asked her. "You'd know, since you've been there."

Elise smiled. It was true, she had been to Paris. In fact she'd traveled all over Europe. The little girl who lived with her grandmother and never left her home state was now well traveled. Her life was completely different from what it had been twelve months ago when she was still working at Curtis Cleaning Products. Those days felt like a lifetime ago, like they belonged to someone else.

Elise had enjoyed a whirlwind of success, and she was loving every minute and didn't want it to end. It all hinged on how well "Endure" would be received. At every turn industry insiders kept telling her it would fail, that it was a bad idea to team up with Dylan Cornish, that he'd tarnish her reputation.

"We're ready for you," a woman with a microphone attached to her head and holding a clipboard came over and addressed Elise. She looked harassed. Elise nodded. It was her turn to go and perform for the video.

"Break a leg," Dylan teased as he planted a soft kiss on her lips before letting her go.

Elise had to wander forlornly along the Parisian streets, wearing a long, beautiful dress. She sang directly to the camera for the first part of the song, and Dylan was filmed separately singing his part. They came together for the final third, encouraged by the director to openly flirt with one another in an attempt to film the sparks between them.

After seven hours of flirting, walking towards the camera singing and generally hanging around on set, the video was complete.

Rather than being exhausted Elise felt elated. She threw her arms around Dylan and he held her tightly.

"Video done!" she gushed excitedly into his ear.

"Yeah, we nailed it." Dylan kissed her gently on the lips.

"I've got to hand it to you guys." The director came over, wearily rubbing his temple. "When I was given this project I had my doubts but you've got some real chemistry. You look great together on screen. I really hope this works out for you."

"Thanks." Dylan said, shaking the director's hand. Elise beamed up at her boyfriend. He looked so different in his shirt and trousers befitting the 19th-century period of the video. His usually messy hair had been tidied up and styled and he was clean-shaven. His beloved leather jacket was waiting for him back in the dressing room. He looked handsome and intense but he was still Dylan. Elise could still see the crinkle by his eyes when he laughed. Each moment she spent with him she fell even deeper in love. Whether or not their partnership in music worked out she was spending more time with him and that was what mattered most.

***

A month later and "Endure" was released upon the world. Elise avoided the internet for the entire week, refusing to look up sales figures or initial responses to the record. She ignored her online fan pages and nested in her apartment with Dylan. Paparazzi hounded them on a daily basis to try to get a shot of them looking tense or anxious in release week but they didn't give them the satisfaction, they just hid away behind her curtains watching old movies together.

In their bubble Elise almost forgot about the record entirely. She was too focused on being with Dylan. But soon the day came when the Billboard charts would be released. She could hide no more from the reality that this one record was going to make or break her career. If "Endure" didn't chart well, at least top ten, she risked being in great debt to Cloud Records and spending the rest of her natural life paying them back The deal she'd struck meant she needed the record to sell well so that she could pay the label back for the all the promotion they had invested in her and Dylan.

"It will be fine," Dylan reassured her as they curled up on the sofa together and switched on her laptop. She had hundreds of emails demanding her attention but she ignored them all. All she wanted to see was the chart.

"I'm nervous," Elise admitted as she clicked on the relevant link and waited.

"I'm right here," Dylan wrapped an arm around her and gave her a reassuring squeeze. "None of this matters. All that's important is right here in this apartment. We've got each other and that's more than enough for me."

Elise nodded though her whole body continued to feel tense and full of apprehension. She opened the page listing the updated Billboard chart. It didn't take long to locate "Endure." It was in the top spot. They had charted at number one. Elise stared at the screen in disbelief.

"Oh my God," she uttered, reaching out to touch the screen as though it wasn't real, just a figment of her imagination.

Dylan began to search for news articles about the song on his iPad.

"Listen to this," he urged her. "Elise Roberts and Dylan Cornish have created a song so beautiful, so simple and so romantic. Watching these two lovebirds perform together is an absolute joy, as though we are being invited into their private, loved-up world. It is so refreshing to see two committed people come together to create something so special rather than being in competition with one another. This blogger can't wait to hear more from the handsome couple."

Dylan proudly showed the article to Elise.

"It's...amazing." It still wasn't quite sinking in. She looked back at the number one beside her name. She'd done it. This was everything she'd ever dreamed of.

"How shall we celebrate?" Dylan asked, leaning close to gently nuzzle her neck.

"Can we order some takeout and just watch a movie?" Elise wondered.

"Like we have been doing all week, you mean?" Dylan laughed.

"Yeah," Elise smiled shyly at him. "I just want to spend tonight curled up with you laughing at old movies."

"I can safely say this whole fame thing hasn't gone to your head," Dylan declared as he began browsing local takeout places on his phone.

"The best part of all of this is sharing it with you," Elise told him sincerely. "That's why I just want to celebrate our success privately, together."

"I love you," Dylan put down his phone and pulled Elise closer towards him. He kissed her softly upon the lips.

"I love you too," she grinned.

Outside paparazzi gathered on the sidewalk, eager to get a snapshot of the couple who were storming the charts. But they were left disappointed. Elise and Dylan didn't venture out for three more days, and then when they did they walked hand in hand towards the subway which they rode to attend a charity auction over in Brooklyn.

***

Over the next several years, Dylan and Elise got married, won multiple Grammy awards and had their beautiful daughter Melanie. All their dreams, both personal and professional, had come true. Whenever anyone asked them if they were happy, they would answer: "We are the happiest people in the world."

About Kate Goldman

In childhood I observed a huge love between my mother and father and promised myself that one day I would meet a man whom I would fall in love with head over heels. At the age of 16, I wrote my first romance story that was published in a student magazine and was read by my entire neighborhood. I enjoy writing romance stories that readers can turn into captivating imaginary movies where characters fall in love, overcome difficult obstacles, and participate in best adventures of their lives. Most of the time you can find me reading a great fiction book in a cozy armchair, writing a romance story in a hammock near the ocean, or traveling around the world with my beloved husband.

One Last Thing…

If you believe that *A Dream for Two* is worth sharing, would you spend a minute to let your friends know about it?

If this book lets them have a great time, they will be enormously grateful to you – as will I.

Kate

www.KateGoldmanBooks.com

In Love With a Haunted House

The last thing Mallory Clark wants to do is move back home. She has no choice, though, since the company she worked for in Chicago has just downsized her, and everybody else. To make matters worse her fiancé has broken their engagement, and her heart, leaving her hurting and scarred. When her mother tells her that the house she always coveted as a child, the once-famed Gray Oaks Manor, is not only on the market but selling for a song, it seems to Mallory that the best thing she could possibly do would be to put Chicago, and everything and everyone in it, behind her. Arriving back home she runs into gorgeous and mysterious Blake Hunter. Blake is new to town and like her he is interested in buying the crumbling old Victorian on the edge of the historic downtown center, although his reasons are his own. Blake is instantly intrigued by the flame-haired beauty with the fiery temper and the vulnerable expression in her eyes. He can feel the attraction between them and knows it is mutual, but he also knows that the last thing on earth he needs is to get involved with a woman determined to take away a house he has to have.

Love for Dessert

When Anastasia Emmott learns of her best friend's engagement, she hopes that her own boyfriend of three years will propose. But instead of giving her a ring, he breaks her heart by leaving her for another woman two weeks before their anniversary. If that wasn't bad enough, Anastasia receives news that she may be demoted to a terrible position in her accounting firm. She decides that finally, she needs change in her life. She quits her job and, much to the chagrin of her mother, starts up her very own bakery. After several disastrous dates, Anastasia begins to realize that the dating game is much harder than it used to be. But when Anastasia's best friend, Ariana, pushes her to enter a baking contest, she meets Darren King, a handsome baker who has just started at the competing bakery across the street. Anastasia is swept away by his dashing good looks, charming personality and masterful baking skills. What Anastasia doesn't know is that Darren is an undercover agent, planted in the bakery to gather evidence against a drug kingpin that has been operating out of his bakery. When Anastasia becomes involved by accident and her name is put on the hit list of the city's biggest drug gang, there is no one but Darren to save her.

CPSIA information can be obtained
at www.ICGtesting.com
Printed in the USA
LVOW11s1036081116
512116LV00001B/4/P